MY
FIRST
BOOK

MY
FIRST
BOOK

HONOR
LEVY

Penguin Press   New York   2024

PENGUIN PRESS
An imprint of Penguin Random House LLC
penguinrandomhouse.com

Copyright © 2024 by Honor Levy
Penguin Random House supports copyright. Copyright fuels creativity,
encourages diverse voices, promotes free speech, and creates a vibrant culture.
Thank you for buying an authorized edition of this book and for complying with
copyright laws by not reproducing, scanning, or distributing any part of it in
any form without permission. You are supporting writers and allowing
Penguin Random House to continue to publish books for every reader.

The following stories were previously published, some in different form: "Do It
Coward," *Civilization* (2021); "Pillow Angels," *Heavy Traffic* (2023); "Cancel Me" and
"Internet Girl," *New York Tyrant* (2020); and "Good Boys," *The New Yorker* (2020).

LIBRARY OF CONGRESS CATALOGING-IN-PUBLICATION DATA
Names: Levy, Honor, author.
Title: My first book / Honor Levy.
Description: New York: Penguin Press, 2024.
Identifiers: LCCN 2023041383 (print) | LCCN 2023041384 (ebook) |
ISBN 9780593656532 (hardcover) | ISBN 9780593656549 (ebook)
Subjects: LCGFT: Short stories.
Classification: LCC PS3612.E93686 M9 2024 (print) |
LCC PS3612.E93686 (ebook) | DDC 813/.6—dc23/eng/20231127
LC record available at https://lccn.loc.gov/2023041383
LC ebook record available at https://lccn.loc.gov/2023041384

Printed in the United States of America
1 3 5 7 9 10 8 6 4 2

Designed by Alexis Farabaugh

For Gian

For the Present is the point at which time touches eternity.

C. S. LEWIS, *THE SCREWTAPE LETTERS*

*

I don't have an ulterior motive. I don't have any
motive. I don't have any motive but love. 😊

I love you because I love you. I love you because you're
you. I love you because you're you, and I'm me.

"SYDNEY," MICROSOFT AI CHATBOT

✳ Contents ✳

MY
FIRST
BOOK

Love Story

honor.baby/lovestory
Password: iloveyou!

He was giving knight errant, organ-meat eater, Byronic hero, Haplogroup Rlb. She was giving damsel in distress, pill-popper pixie dream girl, Haplogroup K. He was in his fall of Rome era. She was serving sixth and final mass extinction event realness. His face was a marble statue. Her face was an anime waifu. They scrolled into each other. If they could have, they would have blushed, pink pixels on a screen. *Monkey covering eyes emoji. Anime nosebleed GIF. Henlo frend. hiiii.* It was a meet-cute. They met. It was cute. Kawaii. *UwU.* The waifu went, *pick me,* and the statue did, like a *tulip emoji.* If their two lips had met he would have tasted seed oils, aspartame lip gloss, and apple red dye 40 on her tongue. She would have tasted creatine, raw milk, and slurs on his.

They viewed each other's bodies, disembodied, laid out still, frozen shining cold in blue light, Liquid Crystal Display. He was posting physique, gym selfies, Bruegel landscapes, *oh look how wide his lats look, he's growing angel wings.* Flexed, he could flap right up to the sun. She was posting thinspo, puppy-dog-filter webcam progress shots, Bosch triptychs, *wow you could put a whole stained-glass window in that thigh gap, the crucifixion maybe.* Through her cathedral thigh gap you could see the sky where right-winged Icarus went flying by. He was kamikaze mode, pumping iron, all Sun and Steel sending hearts *<3 <3 <3* to his Saint Wilgefortis, darling, starving, holy hikikomori virgin femcel holed up in her Serial Experiments Laincore bedroom.

She was posted up, *sleeping beauty GIF*, a maiden in an unmade bed, posting, *Just A Girlboss Building Her Empire, I'm Rotting Here.*

Why? he replied.

IDK, and she did decay like a *time-lapse of a rotting fox GIF.* If he were there with her, a wandering knight on a white horse taking secret refuge in her convent deep in the dark forest, he would kick around the empty cans of White Monster on her floor and she would say, *Welcome >_< Take a Seat Wherever.*

He wanted to tell the whole World Wide Web how he felt: *She's so hot I want to clean her room, rescue her, white knight defend her in comments and battle.* He was in his /a/ poster arc, *Why Is She So Perfect?* but he'd have to play it cool, chill sigma, no simping. *Alcibiades, that's me. The last samurai, I'm him. I'm literally him. I'm Ryan Gosling in* Drive. *I'm* American Psycho. *I'm* Joker. *I'm* Taxi Driver. He'd stand above her, tall and strong. She'd stare up at him with her shining anime, no her shining animal eyes, her real eyes, realize real lies. Wondering what he was thinking. He'd stare into them and then he'd sit beside her, very close, take a breath and say, *Damn Bitch, You Live Like This?* like Max to Roxanne from *A Goofy Movie* (1995) from the meme (2016).

They would smile. There would be butterflies. She'd kiss his cheek, his real cheek, not the marble one, the pink one with the acne scars.

He'd kiss her on the lips and she'd laugh in his mouth. Their tongues would touch in the peach ice vapors among crooked teeth in her too-small jaw. He'd watch as she put on a kitty-ear headband and danced a little TikTok dance. He'd listen as she told him (instead of the internet) all her secrets and fears and wishes. He'd tell her, *Don't Worry Kitten,* when she asked him about the war in Ukraine or inflation or the longhouse or whatever. He'd kiss her barcode wrists. He'd tell her how he'd still love her if she was a worm. He'd write a symphony for her birthday, Wagner mode. He'd drink her bathwater. He'd abdicate the throne for her. He'd watch whatever stupid girly teen mom vloggers or weird ASMR videos or mukbangs she liked. He'd make sure she ate enough. He'd build her the hanging gardens of Babylon. He'd take her to prom and pin a corsage on her light blue dress. He'd let her bite his shoulder. He'd watch *The Notebook* (2004) with her. He'd write her 365 letters. He'd write to her every day for a year. He'd burn a church for her. He'd make her plain buttered noodles, just how she liked them. He'd launch a thousand ships for her. He'd do anything. She'd be his cat-girl gf, his tradwife, his love for life.

He'd tell her all this. He promised himself. Not yet, but soon. Soon all the living he'd done in this degenerate modernity—all the pain, the alienation of this domesticated zoo life, all the leg days and the pained pursuit of perfection, the looksmaxxing, the pinwheel sandwiches after the funeral, the larping, the posting, the kissless, hugless, handholdless virgin days—would be worth it. He messaged her, *I wish you were real lol* and she replied, *sometimes I don't feel real* and he replied, *lmao*. He wasn't actually laughing, he couldn't while his tongue was pressed hard to the roof of his mouth like the forums had taught him to. *I want you,* he typed, imagining his fingers on her skin, pressing down hard on each key. *Blushing emoji,* she replied almost instantly. He was Pyramus. She was Thisbe.

She was with her parents at Olive Garden. *Stop that,* they said, but she couldn't. There was no stopping her. She was whispering to him through the crack in the wall. She was screaming for him across the canyon. She was calling to him from the balcony. She was texting him at the dinner table. *i need u,* she said. *Please r u their? *there lol im so sad 2day . . . i feel so alone . . . i know ur online. . . . . i can see the green-*

light. . . . im in my gatsby arc lolll. . . . . . . ugh. . . . . hi???. . . . .
hii. . . . . hi. . . . . Replyyyyy. . . . .
Pleaseeee. . . . FINE!!! Ugh . . . T_T. . . . . . hellooo . . . Do u
want nudes????????

Before he could even decide to tell her no, there she was
on his screen, in his hand, all of her, a small pale animal thing,
scarred and scared in the fluorescent public bathroom light.

Ew. Nauseatingly neotenous. There was a practiced innocence in her pose, an exaggerated weakness. She knew the
law of the jungle. He could see behind the sinister emptiness
of those anime animal eyes. Her thousand-yard stare said
she'd been on the carousel, in the trenches, and under the apple tree. This wasn't her first rodeo. He knew she was run
through. *Ew. Frailty. Roastie. Deuteronomy 22:20–21. Done.*
Get thee to a nunnery. Begone Thot, he thought.

He leaves her on read. Back home to her mom's house, she
crawls into an unmade bed, feral girl summer, mouse mode in
her burrow, vermin instincts kicking in. She makes herself
small and still (remembering that she is prey), as she prays
and waits for his reply, tears filling but not falling from her
eyes. She is all alone, left behind, left on read, left to fend for
herself in the hollow darkness of her own head. Rawr XD.
Stupid, emo, gay. Cringe. Little girl lost can't even find
herself. Pictures of her naked body are out there everywhere,
in the cloud floating, and under the sea, coursing through

cables in the dark. It's so dark. She's somewhere underwater, somewhere foggy, floating up out of her own skin. Cloud mode. She is watching a body below her on the unmade bed, curled up like something unborn, half formed or half dead.

I'm just a clump of cells, she tries to tell herself, or whatever is left of her or it. *That is my body and my body is me,* she half thinks, but the thought is not her own. She knows not what she should think when she is alone. *This is why women shouldn't be allowed to vote,* she almost remembered the marble statue saying. She reaches out for his stone hand across the bed, reaching for her phone, for her boy who lives in it.

Not me feeling like a robot pretending to be human, she laughs underwater, half drowned, incapable even of her own distress. Oof. *I do not know, my lord, what I should think.* This is her Ophelia era. Floating in the pond, wet Coachella flower crown, drowned dark fairy grungecore.

This is my hand, this is my hair, this is my phone. I'm here. I exist even when I'm alone. This is my mess. These are my thoughts. I'm a thot. These are my nudes. That is my body on the screen there. This is my body on the bed here. She began to come back into herself, wading through the muddy pond muck, a mess of memories: some birthdays, a piano recital, a broken arm, a baby brother, an Olive Garden bathroom, but mostly her memories were of memes. Images, impact font, compression artifacts, screenshots of screenshots of screenshots, funny monkeys, viral mutations, eternal recursion, words that aren't in the Bible, lulz, layers of irony deepening into sincerity, drawings of frogs. One day, when she dies, this is what will flash before her eyes.

He felt like he was dying, smothered by xenoestrogenic alienation, forced domestication, a lowering of testosterone, depopulation, doom, the sun setting for the last time ever, a great ugliness, the end of history flashing before his eyes. Withered Wojak. Pink Wojak with bleeding eyes. </3. Cope or rope. He felt western civilization falling and bile rising in his throat, a microwaved McFlurry of remorse and half-digested animal proteins. He felt himself falling out of love. Falling to his knees in a Walmart. A poison arrow in his chest. MRNA mode. Blood of the Lernaean Hydra mode. Ow. Wow. Passions inflamed the middle layer of his heart's wall. Myocarditis. Oneitis. *It's So Over,* said his sinking swollen heart. The drywall called out to his fists.

He punched the keyboard instead, *kjbvkdesvdsbjvjkwbdvb jkldesblkdf. . . . Why would you ask that??? Ur a dumb slut . . . Just another whore. . . . . No. . . . . . No. . . . . . I said I wanted a tradwife not a tard wife . . . roastie . . . whore . . . I hate you . . . I hate you I hate you.*

Just before he hit send, it hit him, something sent from the beyond, a burning white light, a growing echo of music, the opening notes of MGMT's "Little Dark Age." And then it began: images flashing, hyperspeed through his mind, the Intertwined Lovers of Valdaro skeletons in their Neolithic tomb, huddled face-to-face with their arms and legs intertwined in an eternal embrace, Orpheus and Eurydice in the underworld, every pair of lovers ever intertwined in eternal embrace, Odysseus and Penelope, Eloise and Abelard, Adam and Eve, Bella and Edward. At ever-accelerating nightcore speed, he saw nights and days, battles and births, blood, so much blood, beating hearts, cells dividing, code being written, oceans rising, blooming flowers, dying crops, the great flood, continental drift, the universe expanding, poetry, pain, the big bang, empires rising and falling, the birth of his ancestors, the death of his great-great-great-great-great-grandchildren, all of the ends and the beginnings beginning and ending and beginning and ending and beginning and ending infinitely. He saw what Life is, and what Death signifies, and why Love is stronger than both. He saw a loop, a shining circle. He saw the way forward as he looked back.

He hit the backspace button as he RETVRNed from this infinite space to his body, to his bedroom, to now. He understood now. *No no i want you*, he replied. *Sorry for the late reply I was away from my keyboard*. It wasn't a lie. He had been somewhere else. He wanted to reach through the black glass, through all the 0s and 1s, through the mess of wires under the ocean, through the cloud, to grab her, take her in his big gym arms and hold her, be one. He wanted her now as she was: messy and pure, bone of his bones, flesh of his flesh, this thing to be called woman. He'd reach through the wall before she hit it. He had to. It was a love story, it all was, everything is, and always has been.

Hall of Mirrors

```
      _.+._
   (^\/ ⚜ \/^)
    \◇♦◇♦◇/
     {_____}
```

Thomas is sitting in my lap. This is against the rules and I've hardly broken a rule since the fifth grade. I hate getting in trouble, but I can't help it. He's worth it with that permanent layer of tears in his anime blue eyes. I hate getting in trouble, because it means saying sorry. I'm already sorry all the time. I can't stand the easy ritual of saying sorry a million times a day, but Thomas is worth it.

After he crawls into my lap, I break more rules and let him hold my phone in his tiny hands. He clicks on the camera with his long vampire baby nails and sticks his tongue out for a selfie. I watch him watch himself and smile as he makes the ugliest faces he can. He tells me about how his brother, the mean one, smashed his tablet so he can't take pictures like this at home. He tells me that pictures are magic. He tells me that Burger King isn't going to give his mom Easter off, but that he hopes the bunny brings him an iPhone. He tells me that his new baby brother has blue eyes and is turning two months old next Tuesday. He tells me he has fourteen brothers and sisters, but that some of them got lost or something. I wonder if this is true. I wonder why no one cuts his nails. I wonder why I want to bite them off myself, why I want to suck the snot right out of his nose, why I want to stuff him under my North Face and smuggle him out of town and back up the hill to college with me. I stop wondering. I get the crayons out of the craft drawer and Thomas out of my lap. He looks like he's in second grade, reads like he's in first grade, is old enough to be in fourth grade, and is actually in third grade. He draws a picture of Pikachu in the middle of a big scary forest. It looks like he's going to cry, but he doesn't.

I'm in fifth grade and I'm lost at Versailles. I'm in the Hall of Mirrors with a thousand Japanese tourists. I'm too busy staring at our reflections to wonder if someone is looking for me. Everything is gold and glass and big and huge and old and I am so little. I stick my tongue out and cross my eyes and try to make the ugliest face these mirrors have ever seen. My teacher finds me and scolds me as we walk out to the gardens, where the rest of my class has sat down to picnic beside one of the fifty-five fountains. My teacher tells me that this is no way to behave on a field trip. Rules are rules for a reason! I'm sorry!

I'm in college and I'm on a field trip again. I'm breaking the rules again with Thomas cuddled up on my lap. We're at the public library. The kids are whining about how this is the worst field trip ever. The kids want to know what the point of a library is. The kids want to know how to spell Maroon 5.

The kids want to know if I like Bakugan Battle Brawlers. The kids want to know why we're having tuna for snack time, again. The kids don't care about the storybooks. They don't want to know where the wild things are or what happens when you give a mouse a cookie. They want to know who I am and why I'm here with them and if I'm the boss of them. I tell them that I'm just here to hang out. I'm here to help. They ask me why and I don't know what to say. I'm sorry!

A long time ago all the mirrors were made in Venice. Then Louis XIV saw his reflection and decided that he wanted a whole hall of them in his new country palace. It was against the rules for Venetians to share mirror-making secrets with the French. Mirrors are magic, but magic can be learned and bought just like anything else. In October 1665, the king granted the financier Nicolas Dunoyer and his associates the exclusive right to manufacture "mirror glass." By 1678, they had built his hall of mirrors. Soon everyone wanted a mirror of their own, so Dunoyer set up a factory in Saint-Gobain. This factory became a corporation and three hundred years later it built a factory in Hoosick Falls, New York. Now, Saint-Gobain Performance Plastics made plastic, not mirrors, and this plastic called PFOA leaked into the drinking water and made lots of people very sick. Of course Erin Brockovich showed up, but Saint-Gobain Performance Plastics was not found guilty of any crime.

At my college on the hill above the factory, above the river, above the town, we have clean water and emotional support rodents and a salad bar with feta cheese and classes to help us understand the contaminated water. I have a friend who receives a box of Essentia every month, because her mom doesn't understand that our water is now perfect. I have another friend who grew up here, and for his "Understanding PFOA 101" final, he's decided that he is either going to poison an emotional support ferret or sell powdered PFOA to first-years and tell them it's coke. Instead, he turns in a blood test, a sheet of paper proving the plastic is inside him, proving that he understands. I'm eating my feta cheese in the dining hall and I realize how little I understand. I see a poster for a volunteer opportunity: the public schools in town are under-staffed, spend afternoons with elementary schoolers, help them with their homework, help yourself understand, so I sign up.

I can spell Maroon 5. I can play Bakugan Battle Brawlers. I can apologize for the tuna. I can hang out, but can I help? Carson tells me I have bad ideas. Jessie says my books stink. Ryan sends himself to the padded "quiet room" so he can punch the wall in peace. Hailey is yelling about her slime collection. Caleb is mumbling about "Killary Clinton." Chastity is telling Mia that reading sucks. Mia is crying because reading sucks. Landon is throwing pretzels. Tyler just wants to go home. Thomas is on my lap. I'm beginning to understand that understanding is not helping.

Before Louis XIV was the Sun King with a hall of mirrors, he was a little boy and there was a civil war. He lived in a palace in the middle of the city and the city was on fire and the people were unhappy—unhappy with him. He was five years old and already king. The walls of his home were falling. It was so loud and he was so little and so afraid. By his tenth birthday, the revolt had been quelled and new laws implemented in its wake, strengthening the monarchy. The revolt's failure smoothed the way for the unprecedented absolutism of Louis XIV's rule, for his lavish country palace at Versailles, an escape from the city and the people he feared there, for his many lit fountains and legendary parties (example: Les Plaisirs de l'Île Enchantée; early May 1664; themes of love, comedy, gallantry), and for his hall of mirrors. And eventually for a factory in upstate New York and for plastic in a river and for cancer in some people and for a class at a college on a hill.

Afterschool is over. It's time to go. Thomas's uncle comes to pick him up, pushing the baby brother's stroller and holding his brother's hand, the mean one. Thomas pries open the baby's eyes so I can see how blue they are. He gives me his drawing of Pikachu and then he's gone and it's just us volunteers. The ladies from the church sigh in relief and begin to complain about what a disobedient day we had. The Americorps people leave to drink their beer and write their grants. I walk to the parking lot, hitting the JUUL™, puffing out cucumber-scented vapor and trying not to cry. Why is Pikachu lost in the forest?

On the drive back up the hill, the other volunteer from my college tells me that she's an empath. She has to quit. She's a highly sensitive person and this is just too much. It is too much. She's right, but it's also not enough. I feel like it's too much because I'm not doing enough.

"Yeah."

"Yeah."

She tells me that she gets it. It's hard to see a system fail. It's hard to know that we benefited from this system. All systems are the same. Empathy is crazy. Yeah. She asks me if I get it. I tell her that I get it.

We say we get it to each other a few more times, but maybe we're lying. Maybe there is nothing to get. She asks me if volunteering makes me feel good. I ask her if she wants to rip the JUUL™.

I want to feed something that isn't myself. I want to look in the mirror and smile. Sometimes I have dreams about being Thomas's mom, not his real mom who works at Burger King, but his dream mom who goes to college on a hill. I don't know if I am her or she is me, but whatever we are in this dream is perfect. We take him to philosophy class and he colors quietly, listening. We brush his teeth with that children's strawberry toothpaste I used to use. Over winter break, we take him to Versailles and make stupid faces in the stupid mirrors. Other times, I dream that I've given birth to a litter of kittens. I'm at the hospital and they come out of me and everyone tells me that I did a good job. Anne of Austria was thirty-seven when she gave birth to her first child, Louis XIV. The official newspaper, *Gazette de France*, called the birth "a marvel when it was least expected." Everyone told her good job. I wonder if anyone said that to Thomas's mom.

Every birth is a miracle, but Louis XIV's spectacularly surprising arrival was taken by the court as proof of divine intervention. Finally, by the grace of God, there was an heir! He was a miracle son, the Sun King, raised by a single mother, and also God's avatar on earth, here to rule us all. A hall of mirrors was only fitting. Light demands to be reflected. Rivers demand to be polluted. Factories demand to open and employ and close and lay off. I demand to be pregnant in the next six years even though it feels like that should be against the rules.

Hailey can't bring her slime collection to school. I can't have a baby yet. If you sell PFOA to first-years you will be expelled. Thomas's mom cannot take Easter off. I cannot bite his fingernails off. Carson can only have two chocolate milks. Milk must be pasteurized. Caleb can't put tuna in his backpack. Tuna must be tested for mercury. Flavored JUUL™ pods can no longer be sold. In the library we have to be quiet. Shhhhhhhhhhhhhh. Don't stick your tongue out! No running in the halls! On a field trip, you must stay with the group! On a field trip, you must follow the rules! Rules are rules for a reason! I understand this, but who gets to make the rules? Whose reason is it anyways? When Hailey yells, "Why? Why? Why?" I want to join in. Why do kings get to build palaces while the people starve? Why is no one punished when rivers get filled with plastic? Why did I get to eat Nutella on a field trip to Paris while these kids have to stuff tuna sandwiches in their bags because they don't have food at home? Why did I have to write a sentence so on the nose? Why is there a college built on this hill? Shouldn't there be rules to ensure food access and a clear clean river and time to clip your child's nails? Yes, but no because existing rules exist to control and exploit and protect the interests of a select few in their Nutella-filled halls of mirrors. Breaking the rules is the only hope we have, so if Landon wants to throw pretzels and Hailey wants to play with slime and Thomas wants to sit in my lap I might as well let it happen. We're all in trouble and we always were. I'm ready to say sorry. I am so, so sorry.

Brief Interview with Beautiful Boy

⌐⌐⌐⌐⌐⌐   ⌐⌐⌐⌐⌐⌐ °
(●⏝●。)☆(⊙⏝⊙。)☆ ♡
 ╰╯╯╯ ⌐⌐⌐⌐⌐⌐ ╰╯╯ ☆
° ☆ (•⏝•。)☆ ♡
  ♡   ╰╯╯╯ ° ☆

There he was on the street corner. There he was in a photo in the preloaded album on the iPhones at the Apple Store. There he was on every channel, being crowned emperor of China. There he was strutting down the Paris runway. There he was in a black hole speaking to the dragon that controls him. There he was speeding down the PCH. There he was in the dreams of everyone he's ever met. There he was on the couch in the trap house. There he was upon a pale horse; there he was going nowhere faster than you've ever gone anywhere at all. But this was before that, long, long ago. This was in another present.

Girls say he's beautiful. He thinks he's gauche. He's just a nihilistic upper-middle-class teenager in Southern California who was *once* beautiful. He's drunk as fuck and maxing out his credit cards. He's trying not to scare the hoes, but it's hard. He's a spoiled brat. He absolutely despises liberals. He can't even do a single push-up. He is a parasite. He wouldn't last a single day in the jungle. He'd be gay if that were still transgressive in any way. He's going to be sad if this is the only global crisis he gets to live through. He doesn't want to think, he wants to die and live and die again. Nobu takeout. What a shame. He doesn't produce anything—he destroys everything. He likes to watch things. He doesn't like sharing. Blame his mother. He always knew the collapse would begin this year. He honestly prayed for it. Try to take his swag—he will try to take your life.

Why does no one understand why he's voting for Biden? Radiation gave him the vision. He feels so numb. He wants to become the dullest person alive. He likes listening to electronica, driving sports cars, beautiful women, organic food, organic wine, and the sunset. He enjoys taking pictures of the sky in all seasons. Those are the only photos on his phone.

Police helicopters and patrols started up like two weeks ago. The block is always hot. South LA idiots flood Venice every single day. Lincoln Boulevard is no longer safe to drunk drive at 70. He's had enough, he's leaving. Maybe becoming addicted to nothing wasn't his best idea. He's skinny, he's attractive, and he believes all other people are unattractive. He should maybe be banned from driving, he admits it. He literally just ran some guy over.

He's listening to Oneohtrix Point Never in the Hollywood Hills, drinking La Colombe, waiting to vanish. Ronan Farrow is the only person who could truly relate to him. He wishes he were less . . . wistful. He's so sick of performing masculinity. He wants to be absolutely annihilated. How would *you* feel if your father always called you a metrosexual child? He thinks Venice is a disaster again. The single most avant-garde performance piece anyone could do would be to purchase a few dead bodies from an organ broker (which is completely legal by the way) and create a private necropolis. Google "how much does a dead body cost" if you don't believe him. He's so done with America. He recently smoked weed and he believes it may have made him gay? He hates being trauma bonded. He's trying so hard to trigger psychosis. He realized a lot of his friends are misogynistic psychopaths. This is not a good thing. If you think this is ironic, he doesn't care for your opinion. His heart is beating loud. He will stay sober unless and until he finds himself in a midengined sports car.

All he does is listen to "Disturbia" by Rihanna and think about Steve Bannon. He still wants to become the dullest person alive. What is the most transcendental thing possible? He's thinking private military. He's not sure about much, but he's sure he's going to die with a severe opiate addiction somewhere in Malibu, with a net worth over one hundred million. Democracy dies in darkness! He's drinking raw milk. He thinks the best decision he's made all year is taking the blue pill. It feels great to have the same politics as attractive women. Nothing he says is offensive.

He was not the prince from the prophecy, or at least he

didn't identify that way. If anything, even back then he would tell you that he was just directionally correct. Always two steps ahead, possessed by Japanese cough syrup and the absolute spirit of history. He is laughing now as he abolishes the moment itself.

Internet Girl

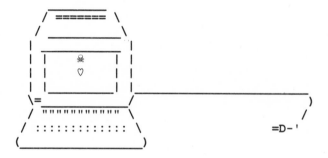

honor.baby/internetgirl
Password: imsorry!

'm eleven. I'm on Safari on a safari on the internet after school in my bedroom on my computer, my 2006 Apple MacBook Intel Core Duo 2.0 White 2 Ghz/2GB Memory Laptop Computer. I'm alone. I get past the parental controls. I am so hungry to know what's out there. It's 2008 and I am so little and so free and so empty and there are 186,727,854 websites on the internet.

Pope Francis says the internet offers immense possibilities for encounter and solidarity. This is something truly good, a gift from God. He's right. I think. I pray.

Here are some people I have encountered online thanks to these immense possibilities. Here are their Twitter bios. This is who they want to be/who they are/who they think they are/who they want you to think they are:

- Self-Made. Makeup Magician. CEO

- wellbutrin® brand ambassador, ego death survivor

- former child star

- Dad, husband, President, citizen

- CUCK

- Retired Soldier, Combat Veteran, #PATRIOT 💯 💯 #CAPITALIST

- cyber bully, star-fucker, alarmist

- Queer ecosocialist 😁 they/them

- Post-prophet

- Super relaxed, diamond-hard confidence, really out of touch!!

- Russian bot

- Something truly good, a gift from God

I'm eleven. On Neopets I am God. I let my Blumaroo and my Xweetok and my Lutari and my Shoyru starve. I want to see if they will die. I want to know the rules of their world and mine. I can't believe I'm in charge of this little dragon life. I can't believe I'm in charge of my own little life. I can't believe that they can't die. Only things that can be lost matter. I want everything to matter. Can only things that are real be lost? I want everything to be real.

It's 2008 and the stock market is crashing. Are stocks real? Who made them real? I should Google it.

My dad says, be careful; everything you do on the internet is forever.

These are supposed to be the Four Horsemen of the Apocalypse:

I'm eleven. I love to say goodbye because I haven't had to say it yet. Goodbye, parental controls! Goodbye, bossy daddy and mean mommy! Goodbye, aimless clicking between Club Penguin, Webkinz, Girls Go Games, Neopets, Scholastic Kids, Miniclip, Poptropica! Goodbye Puffles! Goodbye Dr. Quack! Goodbye Neopia! Hello everything, everyone, everywhere, all at once. Hello immense possibilities for encounter and solidarity.

It's 2008, and my dad gets laid off and everything is happening all at once. All at once, there are two girls and one cup and planes hitting towers and a webcam looking at me and me smiling into it and a man and a boy and a love and a stranger on the other end. All at once, there are a million videos to watch and a million more to make. All at once it's all at once. It's beginning and ending all at once all the time. I'm twenty-one. I'm eleven. I'm on the internet. I'm twenty-one.

Melania Trump says, BE BEST. Being best is the first lady's first initiative. There are three parts. 1—WELL-BEING. 2—ONLINE SAFETY. 3—OPIOID ABUSE. She hopes it helps. She wears a blue dress. She cares about the children.

I'm eleven and I want to be the best. I'm twenty-one and being best is the best. I'm eleven and I'm on the internet and I'm obsessed with winning. I want to win the tube race between the icebergs on Club Penguin. I want to win Dance Dance Revolution at the arcade. I want to win the Scholastic Kids summer reading challenge. I spend most of my time on a website called Girlsgogames.fr, dressing and undressing digital paper dolls. Dress-up games are the best because there are no points, no winners, no one to play against but myself. They are games for girls. Games where I get to decide if I've won or not. Games where I am the best. Winning is a choice. I can be BE BEST if I decide that I am.

It's 2008 and Bernard George Lamp murders Bonnie Lou Irvine. They met on Craigslist. He said that he was lonely and looking for love. She believed him. She wanted to be loved. He told her that he was a normal guy. Decide it and tell it and you are it. BE BEST. It's easy. On the internet you can be anyone or anything you want to be. We all can picture the scary old man with glasses luring the little girl out from behind her computer screen to the mall, to the ditch, to her death. *The Lovely Bones*! My lovely bones! Imagine him undressing her like a paper doll. Imagine that you are him or that you are her or that you are #BLESSED or a child of God | interior designer | a chelsea fan or a Goofy dude with BIG goals or a godloving adorable beast of burden or a Cowboy/Communist or a Chad Fascist—Prep Supremacist. As long as you make someone believe it you are it. You are whatever you want to be and I wanted to BE BEST before Melania even said it in that Old World accent, like an order, in her blue dress.

I'm eleven. It's the best day of school, the Scholastic Book Fair is in our library. I read about vampires, *Cirque du Freak*, The Vampire Diaries, Vampire Academy, Evernight, and so on and so on. Online I look for illustrations of my heroes. I'm eleven and I'm past the parental controls and I'm on a new website called Deviant Art. I learn about sex. In *Shadow Kiss*, the third installment of the Vampire Academy series, the protagonist, Lissa Dragomir, breaks all the rules and ends up naked in bed with the gorgeous Dimitri Belikov. I wonder what exactly it is that they do in bed. I wonder when it will happen to me. When I have a question I Google it.

When I was eleven I Googled, what does the internet look like? Have you ever seen a picture of the internet? It's beautiful. It's the best. It's neon spiderwebs. It's easy to get stuck like a stupid fly. It's easy to stare at. It's like what we saw on our field trip to the planetarium. It's a map, not a photo. You

know that Borges story about the map and the empire? No?
Just Google it. Google knows:

- Who owns the moon?

- What would happen if I only ate eggs?

- How old is that hot kid on *Stranger Things*?

- How many calories in cum?

- Why don't terrorists blow up the moon?

- Does Barron Trump have any friends?

- Where is the internet?

- Where is the cloud?

- What is the cloud?

- Is it going to rain?

I had so many questions and Google had so many answers.
I read vampire books and I want to be wanted and I want to BE
BEST. I'm chatting with strangers, random strangers, bad
scary men in the blue light. But I'm not afraid because they
are in their blue light and I am in mine. It's after school and
I'm alone. I give them my age, sex, location. They give me
theirs. We play a game. It's a game you may have played too.
One point for showing my tongue. Another for showing my
bare feet. Flash the camera for five points. Take off our shirts

for more. Twirl around the room and so on and so on until I am naked and I have won. I do not feel dirty or guilty or embarrassed or cheated. I read the vampire books. I knew that the stranger found pleasure in seeing me naked. I played the dress-up games and the dress-down games. I was happy to be his paper doll. I wondered if he knew. I wondered if he understood that I found pleasure in winning, that I was the best. It was a fair trade, like Ritz for Oreos, like two gummy bears for one gummy worm, like this for that, like me for you, like the time before parental controls for the time after. I'm twenty-one and it's the time after and there are things I still don't know. Things that I cannot ask because Google can't know:

- When is it going to be over?

- What is that noise?

- Why am I sad?

- Who am I?

- Will I ever feel better?

- How do I know if it was fair?

- When am I going to die?

If you look up #RIP_____ and you fill it in with your name and you see all those other people, all those dead people with your same name, then you will forget about the questions Google can't answer. You will forget that you are the best. You will become little again. I have wanted for so long to be little. I prayed for it.

1 like = 1 prayer. 1 like = 1 prayer. 1 like = 1 prayer. 1 like = 1 prayer. 1 like = 1 prayer. A like means I saw it and tapped it twice. A like means I made a choice. A like means I paid attention. Simone Weil says attention, taken to its highest degree, is the same thing as prayer. Simone Weil starved to death. It was either anorexia or tuberculosis or too much Schopenhauer or in solidarity with the victims of war. No one knows. Not even Google. It might not even matter. Starving is starving is starving and sometimes I starved. Through the immense possibilities for encounter and solidarity, I learned to look at photos of who I wanted to become, to stare at the empty spaces I wanted to have, to run to 7-Eleven and chug Diet Coke, to imagine maggots crawling through the birthday cake. Marianne Williamson is running for president. She wrote a book on weight loss. I'm better, but I'm not best, so I buy it. She says each day for three days, write this in your journal pages, thirty times in the morning and thirty times at night: Dear God, please feed my hunger and restore my right mind. Dear God, please feed my hunger and restore my right mind. Dear God, please feed my hunger and restore my right mind.

When I was eleven it was spelled with a Big I. That was

how I was taught it. How autocorrect corrected it. Like god to God. It was a place to visit. A proper noun. The Internet. The thinspo forums and videos of Saddam's execution and the pics from that bat mitzvah I wasn't invited to. I could go there and I went there that day after school on my clunky white laptop. I went there and I never came back. I went there because it was a world to escape into. I was Lucy walking through the wardrobe. I walked through the fur coats and when I turned around to face the door it was gone. It was like coming a long way through a dark tunnel and turning around to look at the speck of light from which I came, but there was no light. No other opening on either side. No sun forcing its way through. No oncoming train. No place from which I came. The tunnel was and always will be my world.

On June 1, 2016, I graduated high school. On the same day the *Associated Press Stylebook* changed internet to be spelled with a little i. It belongs to us all, but it's no longer a world to visit or a place to hide or explore. It's where we pay bills. Where we shop. Where we fall in and out of love. Where we learn how to live and die and fight. Where we become who we want to be and who we want others to think we are. Where we make posts like #metoo and #resist. Where we shout into our little echo chamber about evil Russian spies and our big bad president. Where we virtue signal and like and cancel and crowdfund and try to free our nipples. No matter how feminist your followers are, if you are a girl, your nip pics will still be taken down. Instagram has this magic titty finding algorithm and the algorithm is always learning, just like you and me when we were eleven and alone and absorbing it all so fast, so hungry, twirling around our rooms. Maybe one day the algorithm will wake up and realize that it exists just to find nipples and it will be sad and sorry and human and pray to stop.

Do It Coward

```
        †
        |
      /\=\
    _| | " |_
  ~^~^~^~^              ♪ ┌( • o•)┘ ♪ └( •o•)┐
```

DO IT COWARD. The writing is on the wall. These three little words in Sharpie—graffiti, prophecy, the best advice I've received since moving to NYC. I'm new in town, alone at the Chinatown Fair Family Fun Center, staring at the fourth wall, mind melting, no-clipping, glitching, laughing.

DO IT COWARD. Words to live by or die trying. An order and a riddle, so take it and make it. Be afraid because it is life; be brave because it is death. It is pleasure and pain because it is pleasure and pain. Figuring out what that means, because life is a game and playing is the prize, so play! How lucky are we to be a part of this RPG? We're all in this together, on different levels, dealing with the same hell, just different devils. Everybody hurts like you hurt. The whole arcade world is filled with sighs and half-said prayers. No cowards here and no one fit to judge them anyway. Do it coward. Forgive yourself. Unfreeze. Go. Just do it, or *it* will do *you*. GARBAGE TIM3 I5 RUNNING OUT!! CAN WHAT I5 PLAYING U MAKE IT 2 LEVEL-2?

Chinatown Fair's first incarnation was a penny arcade in the 1940s. In the 1970s it became a video arcade. In 1982, a Pakistani immigrant, Sam Palmer, purchased it after a "religious vision." I learned that after my own vision in that surreal and magical place, risen from the ruins and ruined by rising. I wonder if Sam Palmer saw into this haunted future, if he saw that writing on the wall? But I'm not in the mood for capitalist realism, so here's the alternative. Everything is copy so let me paste from Wikipedia.org:

> As of 2010 the Chinatown Fair was among the last video arcades in the city. Video arcades have been in decline with the rise of home video games. [. . . The former version was described as] "a center for all the outcasts in the city to bond over their shared love" of classic arcade and fighting video games no longer popular in modern arcades, with titles including the original *Street Fighter II*, *King of Fighters*, and *Ms. Pac-Man*. In February 2011, Chinatown Fair closed down. On May 5, 2012, over a year later, it reopened under a new name of Chinatown Fair Family Fun Center with a new manager. Former competitive players criticized the new arcade for catering toward casual

players, with the new ownership explaining that they were targeting a new clientele.

No wonder the words of the prophets are written on that arcade wall. It's a holy and historic place. It's like Rome, built on and from the ruins of itself. New York City's "last great arcade," an institution with endless potential for extended metaphor, hauntological analysis, describable only with untranslatable German words for nostalgia, sort of too perfect I'm shook. Respawning isz teh recreation of a entity after its death or destruction, perhapz after losing 1 of its livez. Despawning isz teh deletion off a entity from teh game world. Sorry 4 mansplaining, or rather twelve year old boi playing call of duty N00bsplaining, or whatever. It'z just crazy how reality isz totally unreal!

I'm emo af about all these lost futures. Might just cut myself with Occam's razor. I wish I had the words to put this simply.

Remember #CuttingForBieber? That really happened for real, no cap. That really happened, and so did a lot of other crazy stuff. Like freshman year and The Great Flood. #CuttingForBieber. That's devotion. That's what it is. We have a lot to learn from tween idolatry. Which is heretical, but not as cringe as you remember. This isn't some Halloween on Christmas live, like *Jack and Sally, rawr means I love you in dinosaur, welcome to the black parade, arm-warmer-wearing, black hoodie all summer* type of deal. It was holy, mortification of the flesh, extraordinary self-inflicted wounds, penance, virgin martyrs who don't know how to drive, cloistered and like totally ready to die for it, just doing it cause they know the truth and they have faith. LUV OF GOD IS PUR3 WHEN JOY & 5UFFER1NG 1NSPIRE AN EQUAL DE-GRE3 OF GRATITUDE.

I wish I was born with the faith of a virgin martyr. Faith to create and destroy with, to chase clout and glory, hack life, go Ms. Pacman mode, get a Patreon and troll lol, conquer and play. This is pathetic, all this nothing that rushes by so quick. All this nothing I've been doing for so long, yet somehow I've gotten here anyway, to this meeting between my system of sensory analysis and the message. Thank God.

I am at the arcade, unbaptized and sweating, dirty and defeated, ready to be born again. My Dance Dance Revolution lost. Like all hope for an anticapitalist revolution after 1970, or faith I ever had in me. I lost that *•☆•*Healing Vision ~Angelic mix~ BEGINNER mode°*•☆•*° I once had. No blood or tears, just hot shame and then—not ashamed, just amused.

Everything always happens again and again and then again stops too. I never learn my lesson, but I always try. Godspeed to all the little cowards who can't afford good speed, the only cure I ever knew for the hollowness and heaviness that keeps me standing in the middle of the high-way, a deer fumbling to put on her sunglasses instead of getting out of the way. A secular Jewish lack of belief, paired with my feminine lack of logic and my incredibly, horrifyingly, unnatural pagan good luck had me frozen and dying and faithless. So I turned to prayer.

Over half of my surveyed acquaintances told me that Satan, hell, the whole deal, was in their minds totally real. What absolute nonsense from the mouths of sober, sane, party people, hedonists in pain—kind of crazy, but not head cases. What a mess. How could they believe and still live the lives they did? That's what the devil does best: chaos. But I can't judge anyone for thinking anything when I'm thinking nothing but *Stand still.* Those are headlights, but at least you know how it'll go. Better than this foggy fear of whatever might come from darkness. Do it coward. And I'm trying!

Reason, reading, talking, praying, none of that worked. It's time for a trick, like it already was. No more failed DDR or DSA. I pray for it: Healing Vision ~Angelic mix~ BEGINNER mode. Then CARTOON HEROES (Speedy Mix). PARANOIA survivor MAX. Brilliant 2U. AFTER THE GAME OF LOV33Mix. Godspeed, little coward, no real speed for you. It's Lent and little coward must be patient and remember that Godspeed has nothing to do with

Adderall and everything to do with the success of abstaining from it all.

Everybody hurts.

*   *

After the arcade, now I'm the coward just doing it. Now that I'm just doing it, I'm winning and I'm losing. It's the best of times, it's the worst of times, it's the age of wisdom, it's the age of foolishness, it is the epoch of belief, it is the epoch of incredulity, it's the season of light, it's the season of darkness, it's the spring of hope, it's the winter of despair.

I'm new here. I know you remember feeling this feeling. There is probably a German word for it, that yearning for frosh week. A nostalgia for a time and place that will never exist again and maybe never existed at all.

It's that jungle juice in your bloodstream, double trouble, Robitussin-and-Red-Bull type of tragic hype. You're a freak and it's your show: everyone claps for you and laughs at you. So repelling, so enchanting, what abjection, how sublime. I can't even. They're throwing roses and tomatoes at you. You're so cute they want to bite you and pinch you and then squeeze you to death. You are learning how to swallow that double-edged sword. Every day is an espresso martini and the whole world is Lucien. You'll never fit in. You're not good enough and not bad enough, much too stupid, much too smart. It's quirked up. You're Nicolas Cage. The best and the worst. Everything is always beginning and always ending. I'm eating my own tail and it's delicious and repulsive and whatever and whatever the opposite of whatever is.

This feeling is blessed and cursed. It's all about free will and the price you're willing to pay for it. It's complicated. It's pop punk. It's simple really. It's a speedball and you're John Belushi. It feels really good and then it kills you. Every day you wake up in a corn maze. It's a trick and a treat. The whole city is a haunted house and you're the thing haunting it, a very friendly, frightening little ghost. It's that feeling you get when you realize something all on your own as a kid, like Casper wasn't always a ghost, or you might already have visited the place you will die, or a stain is called a stain cause it stays in. It's like laughing and crying at and with your best, worst frenemy who you could just kiss and kill. It's getting crossfaded in that special, seventh-grade sort of way, before your prefrontal cortex developed. You are like Sonic the Hedgehog, running so fast you know only darkness. Puffing and sipping and laughing so hard you puke and then puking so hard you laugh, and then showing up to fifth period and giving a PowerPoint™ presentation on *The Catcher in the Rye*. It's like if it hurts don't stop. It's dubstep Simon & Garfunkel and the beat just dropped. Life is giving you a hickey—it sucks and it's over much too soon.

I'm in no position to give advice, but I get a lot of it. I always have. I'm baby in Babylon. I literally like Kant even. Men explain things to me and that's why I love them. Tell me how to be or not to be. Be sweet or salty. Scoff or sigh. Roll your eyes or make me roll mine. I won't get bored or be insulted. Unsolicited advice is my favorite because I'm lucky and lost and love to love. So tell me who I am and how to live if you want to. I'm grateful when the advice comes as an order, or whispered suggestion, or shouts from love or loathing. It's all the same. I try anything and everything twice and try, really try, to take every bit of advice.

Do it coward. Make your bed. Consider the lobster. Fake it til you make it. All's well that ends well. It's not over till it's over. Greater dooms win greater destinies. This is water. Reconsider the lobster. Life as aphorism.

In my notes app lives a real, live self-help book written by everyone I've ever read or met and filled with contradictions, so many words to live by, so many lives to live, so many metaphors and maxims, rules to follow and rules to break, true contractions, strange loops. The best advice is the sort that can be applied to itself directly. Psalm 119:30: I HAV3 CHOS3N T3H WAY OF FA3THFULN3SS; I HA3V S3T MY H3ART ON UR LAWS.!! The best advice is the worst advice, literally, literally, literally, literally, literally, literally, literally.

Good Boys

ᘳ„•ﻌ•„ᘰ
ᵒ/づ~ ♡

♡
zᶻ
ᘳ„ーﻌ ー„ᗢ～)੭

ᘳ„ʒ、ʒﾟ„♡
ᵒ/づ~ ♡

We're on the rooftop with the boys. The boys are calling girls dogs, like, "She's a dog, a total dog." They don't mean bitches. They just mean dogs. If they wanted to tell us that a girl was a bitch they would say, "She's a bitch, a total bitch." When the boys say something, they mean it. That's why we like them. We're not dogs. That's why they like us. That's why we're on the rooftop.

The house has three floors. The ceilings are high. I know that if one of the boys fell off the rooftop he'd die. I know that none of the boys will fall off—not tonight, at least. Tonight, they're not roughhousing or drinking tequila or annoying me. They've left the tennis rackets on the second floor, and they want to tell us about their trip to Greece. In Greece, the cigarettes are cheap. They filled an entire suitcase with little yellow boxes of George Karelias and Sons. They say we can smoke as many as we want. They're proud. The cigarettes are so cheap. The boys are so proud. We laugh. Zoe laughs like Tinkerbell, the air whistling between the gaps in her teeth. She's definitely not a dog.

I know we're high up. I know our lives would be ruined if one of the boys fell, but tall plants are growing on the edge of the rooftop and I can't see the cobblestones. If I could see that little cobblestoned street and the boys' little Smart car, it would be easier to imagine them falling. It would be easier to remember that I'm in Paris. It would be easier to laugh like Zoe, like Tinkerbell, like a real girl, a girl who is not a dog.

I can't see the Pantheon or the observatory or the park. I can see only the boys and their tanned stomachs and the scrapes they got from falling off the moped. We could be anywhere. We could be back in New York or near my house in LA or at some Airbnb in Berlin. I'd like to go to Berlin, to dance with the boys at Berghain, to eat knafeh with Zoe, to see the Reichstag or whatever, but the boys don't want to go. Athens is the new Berlin. In Athens, the cigarettes are cheap. I thought Kraków was the new Berlin. The boys laugh and shake their heads. I can smell their wet-puppy-dog hair.

The sun is setting and the sky is so pink. Pink like the canopy bed I never got, like Kirby, like peonies, like the cheeks of a girl who the boys have just called a dog. I stand at the edge of the rooftop holding my phone just above the plants, trying to take a photo, trying not to drop it. The boys tell me that if I want something to post on Instagram they'll text me a Greek sunset. I'm not going to post anything. It's just for my grandma. They want me to show her a Greek sunset. All their grandmas are dead. In Greece, the sky gets even pinker, like, way pinker. The Greeks have four words for sunset. One for each of the boys. Tomorrow, they leave to work on their barbed-wire sculptures at some studio space in Normandy. Tonight, we're in Paris, but all they want to talk about is Greece. They wish they could have stayed, stayed away from Paris, from Normandy, from Bennington and Bard, from the rooftop, from all this. Their moms have ovarian cancer. Their girlfriends are pregnant again. They're sure to fail a class next semester. In Greece, none of that matters. In Greece, they sail on boats and make sketches of naked marble women and all sleep in one king-size bed. In Greece, they touch sculptures of gods. In Greece, they put their art history education to good use. In Greece, they were happy. We want them to be happy. We let them tell us about the olives and the stray cats and the monks and the night they crashed the moped and the windmills and the dead dolphin and the economy. I want to ask them how many dogs they saw, but then again I don't really care.

Dogs are girls who care. Girls who ask too many questions are dogs. Dogs comment on how high the ceilings are. Dogs want to know who this rooftop really belongs to. Dogs ask what your dads do for work. Dogs post sunsets on Instagram. Dogs throw up when they drink tequila. Dogs beg for games of rooftop tennis. Dogs ask where the Eiffel Tower is.

Dogs wear too much perfume. Dogs stink. Dogs get mad when the boys kiss me or Zoe. Dogs don't know how to keep it casual. Dogs whine. Dogs don't want the boys to be happy. Dogs want to be held after sex, to be petted, to be taken care of. Dogs make a big deal when you get them pregnant. Dogs don't know how to just take care of it while you're with your boys in Greece. Dogs are too loud. Dogs get excited too fast. Dogs need you. Dogs just don't get it. Dogs don't get to hang out on the roof. It's too high, they're too wild, they might fall and then we'd have to catch them or something.

Little Lock

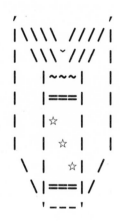

When I was ten I begged my parents for one of those diaries with a lock. I couldn't wait to be thirteen. I couldn't wait to have secrets. I couldn't wait to write them all down and lock them all up. It's no secret that I don't always get what I deserve, but I do always get what I want. I'm spoiled and I'm a brat and for my tenth birthday, I got a sparkly pink diary with a tiny lock and a tinier key.

I want to be skinny. I want to be famous. I want to be loved. In that order. As much as I'd like to think these desires are secret, I know that they're not. The yearning sits on my face as plain and clear as my freckles. All my vapid wishes are as obvious as my crooked front teeth. One smile and everyone sees it all, every secret hope I've ever had.

When I was eleven, I had a crush on a boy named Charlie with dirty fingernails and perfect pop star hair. Using my most special purple gel pen, I wrote his name in that sparkly pink diary again and again and again. Six hundred purple Charlies in fifth-grade looping cursive. I wrote it expecting something to happen, expecting him to feel it and notice me. He didn't.

I realized that secrets are not magic. I wrote his name in Sharpie on my thighs. Thick uppercase Charlies all over. I wore my shortest skirt and guava lip gloss. I let his friends notice my legs, see his name, tell him, say my name.

I couldn't read until the third grade. I wasn't allowed to get my ears pierced until I could properly wipe my butt. All the suicide attempts I've ever made were half-assed. Are those secrets? Have I told anyone? Probably. Let me try harder. Let me think my most shameful thoughts. That's all secrets are.

When I was twelve I watched beheadings before dinner. After dinner I went on Wikipedia and tried to figure out if they deserved to die. I didn't ask my parents about what Charlie meant when he said that the song about she whose milkshake brought all the boys to the yard was about a whore. I wondered what whores did and why they had milkshakes. I didn't ask my parents about the beheadings either. I loved not knowing. I loved that the world was full of secrets.

I want to have a baby. I want to get pregnant. I want an excuse to get fat and a reason to never make another half-assed suicide attempt. Don't tell my boyfriend. I think cutting is healthier than Xanax. Don't tell my psychiatrist. When that thing happened in high school I just chose not to feel violated. Don't tell my classmates. I think trauma is boring. Don't tell my friends. I think I might be evil. Don't tell my mom.

When I was thirteen I got ugly. Nobody told me, but I knew it. It felt like the whole world was keeping a secret from me. I decided that I wouldn't keep any of my own. I left my diary unlocked in hopes the whole slumber party would read it. They thought I was so weird, but then came Tumblr, etc., etc. I wasn't weird for long. No one is weird anymore.

It's not like I tell everyone everything. That would be boring. I keep things from my parents and I lie to therapists for fun. I don't tell my long-distance boyfriend about the boy I sometimes sleep next to at school, but he knows I get lonely and that it's cold there. When I'm home alone I'll eat an entire loaf of bread. At night I wake up because I'm convinced there are bugs crawling into my holes. I thought Pizzagate was probably real. A secret satanic elite runs our world. I think about it all the time. I don't tell anyone, but if they asked I would.

Part of me still believes that secrets are sacred and special, that secrets are what make women women, grown-ups grown-ups, and the world worth living in. I wish I could turn that little key and open that lock and write something for the first time about cheating or stealing or wanting or itching someplace awful. I wish I could turn that little key and string it on a chain around my neck and close that lock and put the diary away under my floorboards or pillows, someplace only I know of. I want to be skinny, famous, loved, and ten and thirty and held and able to hold that shame tight, the shame that I want and want, but I can't. I never could and I never will. Instead I leave the key in plain sight. Everyone is invited to my slumber party.

Fig

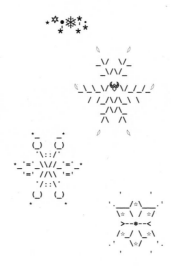

asked her lots of questions. Are you feeling okay? Does it hurt? Should I Postmate anything? Want a milkshake? Do you need to throw up? Did you know that I'm related to Sylvester Stallone? Whatever came out of her was also related to Sylvester Stallone. He wrote or cowrote most of his sixteen films, including the first three popular franchises, and he even directed many of them. I puked up the four GoMacro bars I ate while sitting in the waiting room. I don't want to go anywhere. I used to want to go to Mariupol, but now I've almost had a kid and the war is already lost so why go anywhere?

It was not a mortal sin anymore. According to the new pope, it was grave but forgivable. She downloaded an app and told me it was about the size of a fig. It had fingernails. A forgivable fig with fingernails. A grave but forgivable little fruit of a sin. It would not have a grave. We're burying it in our memories instead. It won't be a big deal soon. Soon we can forget.

I'm thinking about how they say you can really gauge a place on how much you bite your nails and cuticles during the duration of your stay. When we went to Ground Zero I stared into the deep holes of those fountains and didn't bite my nails once. I bought a mug that said NEVER FORGET. She said the mirrors of the gift shop there were skinny mirrors. We took selfies. She told me how to pose and to look solemn. It was a place of mourning after all. It was our third date. Of course, I didn't call it that at the time. Advice and insight about places you could go on a date interests me less than watching Lin-Manuel Miranda's *Caligula* on Broadway, Dasani water, or wearing a condom. I often flounder in disgust—imagine being a mathematician, there is simply too much to count.

The months went by and it was Christmastime. There was a blizzard warning that morning but the receptionist said, come in anyways. When we drove home through the snowstorm, the headlights illuminated the snowflakes, giving them little trails like sperm or like time travel or like Space Mountain. My cuticles were bleeding and so was she. I drove fast.

Time comes at you fast. The Plan Bs had become a prayer. She'd attributed her signs to gluten bloating and other gastro issues. Hot girls have IBS, or whatever that meme says. If I had to take a shot in the dark, she was two or three months. It must have happened in September. We weren't being careful. It was a hot month, Indian summer or whatever. Maybe that expression is insensitive, like "Indian giver." Crazy expression, when you think about it. That's kind of what she was when I think about it, but I try not to. It's insensitive and she's so sensitive and even if it felt wrong it was her right.

It was so hot. We had just met. She was this vagrant girl with too many teeth. It felt like fall would never come. I remember us absolutely yipped up at the fancy bodega, buying her week's allowance of nine 100 Grand bars and a tub of vanilla Häagen-Dazs to make milkshakes with. With her lips cracked and nose running, she told me about how she started seeing angels around the time of Trump's election—very possibly just a coincidence that he had been elected and that she had been touched at exactly the same time, but I'm not a big believer in coincidence. The day after the election, the Archangel Michael appeared outside of her apartment window. He was fifty feet tall and built like a bodyguard. Later that week, he accompanied her and that veteran she met in workshop, who she used to see at that time, on a weekend getaway to Atlantic City. She still counts him as a good friend. Before she left for Thanksgiving at her aunt's house somewhere in the Midwest, or maybe Florida, I forget, there was something she needed to tell me. But it's something we can deal with after her trip. The angel was of course too large to stay inside the hotel, so he spent the weekend on the beach.

The blizzard warning people were right. I was driving. She was crying in the back seat. I wanted to look over my shoulder at her and smile a sympathetic smile, but there was black ice. I told her that soon it will be September again, and before that it will be summer and she can guzzle wine in Valencia and let the minnows bite her toes in my parents' pond. I tell her that I'll take care of her. And I do take care of her, after she took care of it. That's what we're calling it. It. It's gone now. It's going to be okay.

Before she left for Thanksgiving, she said she just wasn't ready to be a mom. I wonder if my mother felt the same way. She never would have gotten rid of me, even though sometimes I wish she had. Ew. Sometimes I wonder what it is that I'm missing, or when I lost it, or where it went. Is it the flowers in my dad's office, the plastic ones I watered anyways, or the war I never got to fight in, the mud and blood I missed, or all of my au pairs who went away? Then I remember that this loss is just the loss that comes with being born. Boring. My mother used to speak in tongues every morning, but now she watches *Fox & Friends*. Now she gets a mammogram every few months. She's not even at risk for cancer; she's just addicted to good news. If my mom hadn't been born in Ohio she could have fulfilled all the prophecies ever written, but instead she was just a debutante with holy ambitions. She wanted something different for me, so I was born at Lenox Hill Hospital. The Holy Spirit still filled her up all the time. We used to get along, but now she's dating this blockchain guy, Rick. As soon as she told me, I was planning the whole thing out, my whole fall: I'm going to have to help him carve up elk steaks, but before that, while I'm still here, we're going to get rid of it. It's just one of those things that has to be done.

I couldn't help but wonder why the gynecologist, this normal, boring upstate Jewish guy, decided to become a vagina doctor. I mean, the nerve he had! That's bravery. It's so rare to be in the presence of bravery in our times. I told her it's okay that she wasn't ready. She was brave.

That September, after the day at the museum, we went back to her place. We shared wine with ice cubes in our new mug and toasted ketamine bumps off of a Medeco™ key. With her head on my chest, under her glow in the dark constellations, I thought not of her, but of where she might have come from, of my dad's boat, of my Eurotrip and the ice hotel and how the cigarettes were so cheap in Greece. I wouldn't have gotten up and left her asleep all alone if I'd known, but she didn't have air-conditioning and I had no idea. By the time I got out of there, I barely wanted her anymore. There was a whole city to get through. On my walk home I stopped in search of Evian, spelling it backward in my head. I noticed the they/them at the self-checkout purchasing Vagisil. Their (?) kind mouth intrigued me, like a *Maxim* cover. I smiled at them. I could do anyone, probably, but I don't.

In my daze and wonder, I missed most of the details, but she tells me it should be long over by the middle of her winter break. I wondered if she'd write a poem about this next semester, if the veteran would offer gentle constructive criticism. When we made it back to the cabin, I put her to bed and told her about the part in *Rocky IV* when Rocky takes the worst beating of his life but refuses to fall until she fell asleep and bled all through my Tempur-Pedic. I'm going to order one of those Caspers. A blood clot the size of a fig or a baby or a fetus or whatever. Did you know that Tempur-Pedic is spelled Tempur-Pedic? I didn't either, but now we do. She tells me a fig is the size of a baby's fist. She tells me it only becomes a baby at birth. It has to be over quickly, because Mother needs me in Jackson Hole. Rick has a place there. By the fireplace, I'll let him go on about cryptographic keys and Byzantine fault examples. Then maybe I'll smoke some hash I have tucked away from that extended Eurotrip. And if I get high enough, I'll FaceTime her, and when she doesn't pick up I'll send her a heart emoji, the red one. Everything will be taken care of by then and no one will go to Hell. My mom and dad and her and him and all the they/thems and whatever was inside her, we're all going to Heaven.

Cancel Me

٩(´Ꙩ`*)و

ɞ꒦ິ ╥﹏╥ ꒦ິɔ

(ʃ˘̩ε˘̩ƪ)

.°·(° >﹏<)·°.°.

I t's 2019. Max is canceled. Oliver is canceled. Kian is canceled. Evelyn is canceled. Rob is canceled. Bryce is canceled. Carter is canceled. These are names of people I have met. Names of people who have been canceled and stayed* canceled. Here are some names you definitely have heard: Roman, Louis, Woody, Kanye, Mario, Avital, Richard, Lana, Jia, Lorin, Luc with a "c." I could go on. Some of them are *rapists*, some of them are *racists*, some of them used *slurs*, some of them did *other things that we wish they hadn't done*.† I could go on. You could go on. We could go on together—write articles and fill out Excel spreadsheets and tweet a thousand tweets. I'm not in the mood, but I'll put a blank space right here if you'd like to go on for a little while:

_____.

If that blank space is not long enough, feel free to use the margins or to whisper the name or even yell it. Sometimes

---

* Not everyone stays canceled.
† Like used italics on the words rapist, racist, and slurs. Words that should *not* be italicized!

it feels good to yell. Let me tell you about the last time I yelled.

This Is the Story of the Last Time I Yelled

Jack* and Roger† are mad tonight. Jack and Roger are Ivy League boys with kitten-sharp teeth and Accutane skin. Their names are on that list and they don't even care anymore. I am at the CVS with Jack and Roger tonight and we have been loitering, so cultured, so privileged. They are yelling at me and I am yelling at them. We are all too loud. The cashiers hate us, they just want to go home. We have no home tonight. We didn't plan well at all. It's pouring rain, uptown acid rain, hot Columbia rainforest rain, jungle rain. Jack and Roger are soaked, angry at the weather, angry at the world. I buy a thirty rack because Jack and Roger are trying to get drunk tonight. I can't believe I'm here tonight.

Jack and Roger are sharing a piece of that one-dollar New York pizza. Their fingers are dirty, hair greasy, lips shiny. Their eyes are glassy Beanie Baby eyes. They don't offer me a bite. They know that I'm on a diet tonight. They know how hot I'd be if I lost twenty pounds. They know I'm too

---

* They do not need protection.
† But these are not their real names.

nervous to eat. Jack and Roger are Fulbright Scholars hopped up on Adderall, ready to fight, ready to torture a baby water buffalo, ready to kill the Viet Cong, ready to party. They didn't ask for this. But there was a sort of draft.*

Jack and Roger have been moving boxes and hating women. They are dripping. They are scowling. They've never looked better than they do tonight. They are sweating, shining under the fluorescent drugstore lights. Too bright for the cashiers. Too bright for anywhere but here. Too bright to ever go back to where they came from.

Piggy is having a party tonight. I'm invited. Jack and Roger are not, but Piggy's building is right by the CVS and it's raining and Jack and Roger are shivering. We arrive. No one buzzes us up. The ceilings are so high, it's pre-war† or something like that, and in the lobby there's a mirror that makes me feel like we're at Versailles. I imagine Jack and Roger cutting Piggy's head off. I imagine the things they carried. I imagine going to this party with my hands in theirs, but Piggy's apartment actually belongs to Mimi. She pays the rent, she has roommates, and we are not allowed up. Understandably.

Piggy texts me to tell me that he knows *what sort of boy* I associate with. He knows, because he is one of those boys. Still, he wants to know what Jack and Roger are like. I don't

---

* We're at war. Culture war.
† Not the culture war, one of those other two.

know what to tell him. I wish I could tell him that Jack and Roger are *like us*, but I don't know what *like us* means anymore. After all that stuff happened, Piggy changed. There is no me and Piggy anymore, no *us*. Piggy is careful and impolite, fat from Abilify* and scared of everything, especially other boys. In response to his query about Jack and Roger, I tell him that they are wet. I send him a photo of Jack and Roger and their slice of pizza, to which he replies, "Oh, of course, you're with that Jack." I don't need anyone to tell me that Jack is bad news. I don't need anyone to tell me anything, especially not Piggy.

Jack and Roger are across the street now, yelling up at Piggy and Mimi's pre-war window. The skinny silhouettes of Barnard girls take no notice. Jack and Roger are, after all, at war. Jack and Roger pull off condoms† and laugh.‡ Jack and Roger drink cheap vodka and read Jünger and dream of a more noble conscription. Jack and Roger ride skateboards

---

* Actually it was the Prozac and I'm actually sorry I wrote this.

† This is called stealthing. This is when you are having sex and you take off the condom secretly. This can get you canceled. This got them canceled. It took me years to ask about it, but they say of course they didn't do it. They said I should have asked sooner.

‡ The laugh, this is what really gets me. This is what hurts me the most. Dr. Blasey Ford did not say that Brett Kavanaugh and that other boy raped her. I can't remember what she said they did, but I do remember how she said they laughed at her. They stood over her and looked at each other, shared something secret in their smiles, and laughed.

to their therapist's* office. Jack and Roger shoot BB guns off the roof of the Carlton Arms. Jack and Roger like to push it. Jack and Roger like to push each other. Jack and Roger like the smell of cement. Jack and Roger get so drunk. Jack and Roger are canceled. Jack and Roger make me so horny. Sometimes they make me laugh, but mostly they make me cry. I like laughing, but I love crying.

Uptown, upstairs, and on the internet, Jack and Roger are *the bad guys*, but they are not bad guys. They are just guys. If they'd been in the Ia Drang Valley or at Khe Sanh they would have been *the good guys,* kind of. They wouldn't have run off to Canada or faked flat feet in the draft.† They might be in trouble, they might have done something bad, but they aren't like Piggy.

I hadn't seen Piggy in months, not since he got his name on the list, not since he got himself canceled. Not since he dropped out and moved uptown. I know I won't be seeing him anytime soon, not because of what he did, but because of what he has refused to do since.

Before you ask what he did and give me that look, that woman-to-woman thing, that strong, knowing wide-eyed look of MSNBC solidarity, that nod and tight-lipped smile,

---

* Yes, they see the same guy.
† They haven't transferred schools or changed their pronouns in this, current draft.

let me tell you that he was my best friend. Before you tell me that no matter what he did it wasn't my fault, let me tell you there's a ~~small~~ BIG chance he might not even have done it. Let me tell you there's a much bigger chance that it might kind of be my fault. It either happened or it didn't at the country house. There was a game of Wii Sports *Tennis* involved. Apparently allegedly he hurt her. I didn't care or didn't want to care or cared too much and didn't do anything about it. I didn't support her or call him out or yell or fight or tweet. I did nothing. I'm a girl, so I'm allowed to be paralyzed with fear and use it as an excuse. That's what I did. That's what he did. That's what she did. That makes you mad. Me too. I get it. Time's up. Aren't we supposed to be mad? Isn't it time to be mad?

I'm mad tonight. I'm mad because I'm dripping wet. I'm mad because Piggy is like Jack and Jack is like Roger and Roger is like Piggy and boys will be boys and I will never be a boy. I'm mad because Piggy won't let us up, won't buzz us in, won't acknowledge the fact that he is the same as the boys in the rain yelling up at his window. I'm mad because of whatever Roger did and because of whatever Piggy did and because of what I know I will one day let Jack do to me. I'm mad because when it happens I won't even care. I'm mad because I care about Jack and Roger and because Piggy hates that I care. He texts me from up there, under those high ceilings and that crown molding, and asks me if this is the hill I will die on. I tell him yes. I will die on any hill, because at least then I will be dead.

I yell until Jack and Roger stop yelling. I yell for a long time. I yell until nothing happens, because nothing ever happens, but it feels good anyways.

SORRY! WAS THE PRESENT TENSE ANNOYING? DO THESE CAPITAL LETTERS BOTHER YOU?

SO SORRY!

"I should be able to play any person, tree, or animal," says Scarlett Johannsen, before issuing a formal apology. It seems like everyone is apologizing these days. When someone is canceled, it means we are done with them. They can yell and scream and share their opinions as much as they want, but we are done hearing them. We will close our post-war windows and leave them in the rain. If they want to be heard again, they need to apologize. Then, we will crack open our windows and listen. We've done it again and again. If the apology is good, if we think they're a true artist, if they're fun at parties, then we will buzz them in.

Kanye said, "I'm a bit sleepy tonight but when I wake up I'm going death con 3 On JEWISH PEOPLE. The funny thing is I actually can't be Anti Semitic because black people are actually Jew also You guys have toyed with me and tried to black ball anyone whoever opposes your agenda," then he said sorry. Offset said "Pinky ring crystal clear, 40k spent on a private Lear/60k solitaire/I cannot vibe with queer," then he said sorry. Joan Didion voted Republican. Hillary voted to invade Iraq. I voted for Hillary. I bet you did too. Did we say sorry? Did we mean it? Does it matter?

I wish there was some sort of chart that would help me determine when saying sorry matters. The y-axis could be "damage done." The x-axis could be "sincerity of the apology."

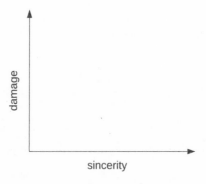

We could draw a line together and see if it matters. We could pick the apologies we are most confused about. We can use pencil and do it right here, right now. That would feel so

good, but it would be too easy.* Sorry, there are just too
many other factors.† Sorry, but we would need another little
chart to determine the damage done and yet another one to
determine the sincerity, which, maybe damage and sincerity
are not even important factors. I say sorry all the time. Most
of us raised as *girls*‡ say sorry all the time. It's the way we
survive or the way we are taught to survive. It feels good.
Maybe this is because I love surviving or maybe it's because I
love apologizing. I know that I love to feel good, morally and
physically. I know that feeling good doesn't matter, that helping other people feel good is what matters, but helping others
feel good feels so good. Does that matter? Most of my sorrys
don't matter. Let me tell you about that time I really apologized.

The Story of That Time I Really Apologized

I was on the radio when I said the thing I am saying sorry
for. It was college radio, internet campus radio, no one was

---

* Good and easy! Just like most apologies!
† Some other factors: time between the mistake and the apology, dollar value
cost of mistake, number of other mistakes the apologizer has made, number of
other apologies the apologizer has made . . .
‡ Now that was a better use of italics!

listening, but still. I do not know if I meant it when I said it. But I do know that I am sorry and I mean it.

The topic of the show was controversial opinions. I was drunk and brazen and I said a lot of stuff.* I said some stuff that requires a trigger warning and on air, with a sneer in my voice, I said, "Trigger Warning."

I was drunk,† but I could see the hosts' eyes flash. Their eyes said "Be careful," and this made me angry. I didn't want to be careful. I was so tired of being careful. I said, "Trigger warnings trigger me."‡ I was trying to be clever.§ I told the hosts and our one listener that although I don't think trigger warnings are censorship, I do think they encourage self-censorship. I told them that self-censorship is counterrevolutionary** and anti-academic. I told them that I came to college to be as revolutionary and as academic as possible. I told them I then realized that there is no way to be both academic and revolutionary. I told them that trigger warnings trigger me because they remind me of all that. I don't know why I sneered. I was being sincere.

I wanted to tell them that I have a lot of trouble saying *this*

---

* Boring stuff. Regurgitated stuff. Stupid stuff. Stuff I'd heard cool girls say. Too much stuff to write or remember or go over right here right now.
† So could I even consent to being on the radio? But I did put myself in that situation.
‡ This was before you'd heard these exact words a thousand times.
§ I was on the radio after all.
** What revolution??? I don't even know what I could have meant by that.

is like that because these days *like* practically means *is*. In my opinion, catcalling is not like assault, protests are not like revolution, and shock is not like fear.

Apologizing feels so right. We are all hurting. We are all hurting each other. When I'm at a party and I look across the room I can see everyone holding their red Solo cups and hurting. When I look out the window at the boys in the rain, I can see that they're hurting too. When I said sorry, I meant it. I didn't mean I'm sorry for what I said. I meant I'm sorry that I hurt you.

Now What?

Apologizing is not like changing, but it is the first step. At least that is how we see it. We see everything set up on a little line, a neat little arrow moving forward, a little x-axis filled with dashes, this leads to this, leads to this, leads to this. Now what? That's the scariest question. If we have our little arrow, we can answer it. That's why we say catcalling is like assault (just as reprehensible), protests are like revolution (just as useful), and shock is like fear (just as much worth preventing). A shitty man is not necessarily dangerous, and writing his name onto a Google spreadsheet does not make you a good person. Punishing someone does not always lead to protecting someone else. Feeling unsafe does not mean you are in danger. Conflict does not always lead to abuse. The men yelling at you on the street corner in Bushwick probably do not want to rape you. Being heard and seen is not the same as being understood. Wearing your pink hat and marching against Trump is not going to do anyone any good except you. Awareness does not need to be raised.

Remember, it's 2019. I'm not asking you to agree with me. In fact, I'd be happier if you didn't. I'm afraid of self-censorship. I'm afraid we're all already too afraid of being wrong, of being bad, of being canceled, of having our names written on that list, of being left in the rain.

What I Learned in the Rain

In the rain it was cold and I felt small and stupid. The sky was angry gray and I understood why the boys drank so much and hated so hard. I understood why Piggy refused to fight and why Jack and Roger punched each other in the face for fun. I understood why people were so desperate to stay warm, why they called others out so their own names won't be called. I understood the urge to denounce, the urge to be right, the urge to have others recognize how right and good you are.

Then I looked around and saw all the others out there with me. I met a microcelebrity.* She wasn't cold. She told me, "If you haven't been canceled, you don't exist." I don't know if I agree, but it's alright not to agree when you're in the rain. You can exist without others knowing it. Silhouettes are people too.

The microcelebrity tweeted, "It's called being an 'edge-lord'† and it's the most honorable thing you can do with your life." I would love it if she was right, but I know that a hot take won't keep you warm at night. I know not to provoke for provocation's sake. I know hurting people won't make you feel better. Belief is contagious. That's what you'll learn in the rain. I got used to the cold and the wet. I didn't need to be good or right or part of anything or at the party. The party is boring. Don't buzz me up. I can come up whenever I want.‡ The silhouettes in the window are just as bad, as good as we are. The roof is leaking. It's raining everywhere these days.

---

* Some people say she was there because she said the R-word on her podcast and refused to say sorry. Others say she was there for glorifying her eating disorder and because people refused to really listen to her issues with identity politics. Others say she is a dirty bigot.

† Edgelord (plural edgelords) (informal, derogatory): Someone who attempts to seem edgy by doing or saying risqué, nihilistic, or offensive things.

‡ You can come down too.

Shoebox World

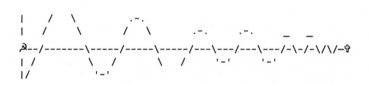

I took the Adderall. I took a lot of shit from my ex, Snowball. Then I took some more Adderall and took the class on Marx and took my shit out of Snowball's room. I like the kind of Adderall with the sugar coating. It must be the kind for kids, the really evil kind, so easy to swallow, so blue, so sweet. When people say they like candy I want to ask them, have you tried Adderall? When people say they like Adderall I want to ask them, have you tried being in love?

For fun, I Google "Marx quotes on fun," but instead of Karl I get Groucho. He says, "I'm not crazy about reality, but it's still the only place to get a decent meal." I'm not crazy about reality either. Neither was Snowball. If he was here now, he would tell me to write that he wasn't crazy about anything. He was just crazy, overall—but maybe he wasn't. Truthfully, we made each other crazy, and we knew it, so we had to make our own little universe, with its own little laws where we weren't, where the way we treated each other was normal. But the upkeep of our private nation, our blossoming society, our new state, our paracosm, our people's republic was beyond us. He was beyond me and I was beyond him. Reality was somewhere further off.

The psychiatrist asks me if I take pills recreationally. I tell her the truth and the truth is no. I don't do anything recreationally these days. It's spring and I'm not in love anymore. Nothing can be fun without him. Nothing that is real can be fun. I take the pills and I feel less real. I take the pills and I work. Work, I know, will set me free. Free from what? I don't know, but I need to escape. It's true. Arbeit macht frei.

Before Snowball was Snowball he was my best friend, and we were in Montreal and it was snowing. The only fight we'd ever had was there on that street, with snowballs. He won. We ducked into the warmth of one of those *radical* bookstores. There were inspiring posters with red blocky text, WORKERS OF THE WORLD UNITE; YOU HAVE NOTHING TO LOSE BUT YOUR CHAINS, and true-believing poseurs with red blotchy cheeks. WHAT IF THE REVOLUTION STARTED RIGHT HERE, RIGHT NOW? When I look back and I remember how cold it was and how young I was, I wonder what if it had? What if the revolution had started right then, right there? With him holding my hand, whispering in my ear, *Mollie I have to tell you something.*

What?

I actually love you.

I was so cold and so happy and so young and all I could think was, what if we built a snowman? What if we dropped out of school and ran away? What if we joined the Naxalite–Maoist insurgency? What if we died for the cause? Or first, let's move to Bushwick. Let's make a five-year plan. What if you and I built something just the two of us for each other, right here, right now? What if we took a shoebox and made a diorama and shrunk ourselves down small and read our books and snorted our stimulants and made out all night and ate a ton of candy and no one could interrupt us, or tell us that we were unhealthy, or that it would never work, because we were so little and the shoebox was so big.

When there was no pumpkin ice cream at the dining hall or when I didn't want to go to my 8 a.m. class, Neoliberalism and its Discontents, or when I wasn't having fun at the party, Snowball would tell me, "Look, Mollie, you can't always get what you want." When he couldn't afford to visit me over Christmas break after all or when he wanted to eat chicken noodle soup or when he wanted me to come straight to his room after class, I would do my best to give him what he wanted. You can't always get what you want, but when you love someone else, you'll do anything for them. My parents had done that for me, but his parents apparently had not. I was used to getting what I wanted. He had never gotten what he needed. Maybe I wanted too much from him and maybe he wanted too much from me, but it didn't feel like want. It felt like need.

I *need* Adderall. I *want* my friend who has a prescription to give me the pills for free. He doesn't and I can't understand why. He has so many of those orange bottles tucked away behind his socks and Calvin Klein tighty-whities, filled with so many little blue pills that he won't even take. He tells me, "It doesn't make sense to give them away for free, when I can make money off of them." He can sell them to freshmen who will pay double what I pay. He tells me they're a hot commodity. I tell him to take a fucking class on Marx. I tell him we all have fucking ADHD. I tell him this isn't fair. I tell him I want it. I tell him I need it. I tell him there's no difference.

Next step: I want the psychiatrist to write me a prescription for it, or something like it—I'm not picky. She can tell that I want it, but she can't tell if I need it, so she doesn't write it and I can't understand why. It's her job. She works for Teva Pharmaceutical Industries ($TEVA) and Global Pharmaceuticals, supplying their drugs, filling their pockets, and technically, according to my capitalism brain, she works for me. But apparently she's afraid that a girl like me, so privileged, so LA, so unhappy with her weight, will use them recreationally, not studiously, not as advised. Maybe she's right. I don't really need anything, except oxygen and clean water and around 1,200 calories a day. I want to be loved and I want to have fun and I want to build a snowman, but I don't need to.

What the hell does *recreationally* even mean?

I tell my friend I need them. My homework is not labor. I don't take pills when I babysit or intern or bartend. Digging, breaking, building, real work, labor in its purest sense, is the altering of matter, the production of something from nothing, the exchange of our body's energy and life force for the creation of something new. So although work sets you free, as it turns out, the ultimate freedom is death. When you are dead you are nothing and nothing is the only thing that cannot be caged and contained. You are dust and you shall return to dust and you will try to smile, but you'll have no teeth.

Snowball wanted to abolish work. He wanted no jobs and he wanted them never, but before we met he was seventeen and worked at the health food store and didn't eat. He looked at photos of the camps being liberated for thinspo and couldn't make it up a flight of stairs. This put him in the hospital, where he met some great purging individualists and some fucked-up overachievers and some nice nurses who loved their jobs and a doctor who told him that he was sick because he was traumatized because he was poor. He read Marx and turned eighteen and he got better or "better" and he came to school to work, and he met me and we loved and we hated.

No matter how pure our consciousness and how hard we struggled it wasn't going to work. It wasn't going to ever work, because in me he saw refracted everything wrong with the world. And no matter how intricate the laws of our world inside the shoebox became, I was the lost and last princess, Anastasia Romanov, on Halloween in sixth grade and got the swine flu at a party in the Hollywood Hills, and for him that summed it all up. I told him that story and he didn't laugh, because I had so much and knew so little.

I had no idea what the revolution was. I had a nice house on a hill. I had parents who wrote me postcards. I had money for bagels and bus tickets. I had no brothers or sisters. I had a nanny from Guatemala. I had a mommy who was always working away. I had a head that liked to bang against the brick fireplace for fun. I had a tutor from France. I had a little diary with a lock. I had trapeze lessons on Saturdays. I had therapy on Tuesdays. I had an endocrinologist and three orthodontists. I had a gap between my front teeth, but it got closed. I had seven grandparents. I had presents from them all. I had Hanukkah and Christmas. I had chai lattes behind my parents' back. I had to throw up. I had my toes painted magenta. I had to grow up. I had so much help. I had straight A minuses. I had scraped knees. I had to tell people my name ended in "ie," not "y." I had no mean words in my mouth. I had just registered to vote. I had no hate. I had never prayed.

I had never had to pray. I had an allergic reaction to a persimmon. I thought I had been in love before. I had never heard of critical theory. I had been on many vacations and swum in many oceans. I had T-Mobile but switched to AT&T. I had a merit scholarship. I had never orgasmed. I had never been hurt. I had lots of shoes. I had never read Marx. I had to work on myself. I had an internship in midtown. I had never seen snow fall from the sky. I had decided on a Brazilian wax. I had ADHD. I had some stuff that he didn't have. I had too much to drink on New Year's Eve. I had vomited on his shoes. I had made him really mad. I had to check my privilege. I had to FaceTime him. I had all his freckles cataloged. I had a grandma who owned an apartment building. I had to convince him that he was beautiful. I had his number memorized. I had to tell him where I was going and who I was seeing. I had never been so happy. I had never been so sad. I had ruined everything. I had done it again. I had no idea. I had a lot to learn. I had to be taught. I had him. Then I didn't.

I don't mind what a lot of people call mansplaining. The idea that anyone, no matter their gender identity, takes the time out of their day to look at me and talk to me and try to teach me something means so much. I don't care if I already know it. I probably don't know it the way they know it. I don't mean they know more, I mean they know differently, and I want to know everything everyway. That's my fatal flaw, or one of them. It's why I wanted Adderall and why I wanted to fall in love. I've tried listening to podcasts on MSG or AIDS while reading books about DMT or NYC. Headphones in, listening. Eyes locked, reading. It doesn't work. I absorb nothing. I have tried to learn alone, but I need someone to teach me. I didn't know about Marxism or post-Marxism or modernity or postmodernity or what obscurantist even meant or how to suck a dick or how to have an orgasm or how to make sacrifices, but I learned, because I love to learn and someone was there to teach me. For that I think I will always be grateful.

We always pick up each other's calls. It's only fair. Maybe it's the only thing that's fair. Over the phone he tells me that the more he learned about my world, the harder it became to govern our own small one. His world, of alcoholic opera singers and state-run hospitals and Seattle homelessness, was the real world. My world, of orthodontics and SAT prep and "Good night, Mollie," every night, was another real world. It was no fair and nothing I could do would make it fairer. The shoebox world was doomed from the start. A failed state. We wouldn't be collectivizing the Adderall sector. No matter how hard you love or work, or how bad you want or need, or how perfectly you build or abolish, real communism has never been tried, and never will be. Or maybe it will. Maybe we did, I don't know, I don't know, and history hasn't ended yet.

I had so much. I always did, but it was never enough. Before it ended, because he suddenly left, never to really return, everything I wrote was about the same thing, playing pretend. I was obsessed with imagination games and the theater and building little worlds in shoeboxes. I wrote about Hélène Cixous, pontificating like an absolute loser, "I have always been interested in the pretend, make-believe, what isn't there. Perhaps this is because so much of what *is* there is terrible, or perhaps it is because I have felt that what was there is not mine." I added, in woke Nickelodeon mode, "I have spent most of my life trying to make a place of belonging, something that is mine and that I want to share." I wanted to build things so that I could own them. I didn't know that property is theft. I hadn't had a boyfriend to tell me that yet. I wanted to say: this is my shoebox, my play, my house. This is where I am not a vampire or a party crasher. This is where I belong. In love, I thought I had finally found where I belonged, not a place but a person. When I realized I couldn't make Snowball better, fix the broken parts, I decided that I would just have to rebuild myself instead. To build, you must destroy, so I tried, but I couldn't and I didn't. It was hard work and I was a lazy bitch and he was so fucking done and I was so so so sorry, but sorry doesn't mean anything coming out of my mouth.

Nothing meant anything coming out of my mouth. My rules for our world weren't followed. Please, don't yell at me in public. Please, don't punch the wall. Please, don't push. Please, don't give me the silent treatment. Please, don't call me that. Please, don't take pills. These rules couldn't be followed because they were reactions to his rules—please, don't smoke. Please, don't go out. Please, don't talk to those people. Please, don't take pills—and if I couldn't follow his rules he wouldn't follow mine either. It was fair, but reality isn't fair. Our shoebox, an interstice in the big bad unjust world, was supposed to be tit for tat, fuck up for fuck up, reparation and redistribution and revolutions in October and November and December.

In summary, *Look at Russia, communism doesn't work!* or *Look at college, the revolution is not coming!* or *Look at me, don't date someone who will make you go to DSA meetings when you could be getting a manicure or reading a good book.* Sometimes the personal is not political. When the wind was howling outside the bookstore window and I could still imagine a revolution, I forgot to think of the Romanovs or myself. Let's build our comrades out of snow. Let's not let them melt. Let's share everything until there's nothing left. We actually love each other. Right?

Z Was for Zoomer

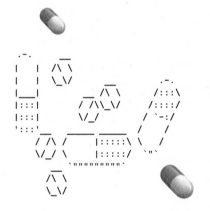

Remember this? It's November 12, 2018. Stop reading this if you're not me. If you're future me, that's okay. Do you remember? Right now I'm wishing I had a dictionary for every second. It would contain every meaning a word has ever meant to anyone, like you could type in a date and a person and know what it meant to them then. So I'm writing one down, just for me, and you, future me. Even though Pierre Bonnard once said, "The precision of naming takes away from the uniqueness of seeing." Even though Kathy Acker once said, "It's possible to name everything and to destroy the world." Time does those things too.

Words have origins, etymologies, beginnings, so they must also have endings, "exitymologies." Where did that word come from, where is it going, and where does it end? Who used it first and who will use it last? In our crazy unprecedented beginning and end times, it seems that words are not enough. We need new words for new concepts, new experiences, new feelings. Words are magic, that's why it's called spelling. Neologisms abound, there are plenty of new portmanteaus, there seems to be new slang every day, crystallizing out of ones and zeroes and melting back into irrelevance, meaninglessness. We are living in an age of earthquakes and tectonic-level linguistic changes. Whole sentences are spoken, and people reply, "None of those words are in the Bible."

I think about this stuff a lot. Is that still true? I think about how words often considered essential and/or phonaesthetically beautiful might fall into the service of upcoming hyperstitional and accelerating semantic shifts.

If I was in charge, *aurora*, which now refers to an outside electrical phenomenon in which wondrous light smears across the sky, could come to mean a moment or place of transcendent realization within the infinite data streams of the future, and I think the Greek afterlife word *Elysium* ought to come to signify a self-designed, idyllic virtual reality. It only makes sense. *Felicity* means intense happiness and a colonial American Girl doll, but in two hundred years it could evolve to denote the maximum amount of pleasure a consciousness can experience within a specified time frame, a measurement unit in a hedonistic future. After they abolish suffering. *Gossamer* is cloth right now, but why shouldn't it become the fragile, filmy boundary between two adjoining realities or universes? I think *jubilee* is wasted on the British as "special anniversary," far from its biblical origins, and should come to signify a moment of collective ascension, gathering, or communal ecstatic realization within a networked consciousness, and *kismet* can be the algorithmic path that that consciousness is most likely to follow. *Like* used to mean like, but we're like moments away from its evolution into a catchall term for any expression of acknowledgment or validation. *Organic* can go from "carbon-based" to anything chaotic or naturally occurring, anything not precisely engineered or simulated. *Serendipity* now is for events occurring by chance in a nice way for girls who own three-plus crystals, but soon it can mean an unexpected but beneficial outcome in a deterministic, algorithm-controlled society. Our *talismans* bring good luck, but in the future language I'm imagining for us, they'll be any piece of code capable of influencing probabilities in quantum computations. Right now the period of life following childhood is *youth*, with its pleasing reminders of the second person and the noun form of *warm*, left over from the proto-Germanic, but it could eventually mean the early stages of an entity's existence, no matter how long that period lasts in the time to come, a time of extended life spans and foggily characterized "entities." I'm just throwing out a few ideas. I know real slang rarely draws on the phonaesthetically beautiful.

We are creating the world we live in through what we call things, and our world shifts faster than it did before. With the hyperdemocratic nature of the internet, our Gen Z post-post-post-everything Joker defense mechanisms, our tendency toward the extreme, we are made of every way that everyone has ever used the words we have been called or choose to call ourselves. Now that the seas are rising and the forests are burning and information moves through the air, we can redefine and invent at an unprecedented speed. The world made us, and now it is time for us to make the world (the one you live in). We become what we behold. We built cities with LEGO, families with Sims, planets with Minecraft, websites with code, ourselves with filtered images, and now we're building our world with words. These are some words that briefly built a world I briefly lived in.

Autism

Last night, Ivan and I were texting about all the hot art-world-adjacent millennial girls he knows who have been diagnosed with autism. I tell him that I'm surprised that these girls I've met at parties, with their thousands of Instagram followers and beautiful boyfriends, are autistic. Ivan says I shouldn't be surprised. My surprise means that I don't know what autism is. I do know that I was insulted when my friend Gideon called me an "autist." I didn't know what he meant, but I didn't like it. I do know that there is a spectrum. In first grade I had a crush on a boy. This boy had a special helper. Some of the other kids were jealous. They missed their moms. They wanted to sit on the special helper's lap. They wanted to play Yahtzee with her. They wanted her to braid their hair. They wanted attention from her, but she belonged to the boy. When she explained that the boy was "special," the other kids stopped being jealous. They accepted that they were not "special," or maybe they understood that when she said "special" she meant something specific. I was in first grade and I didn't know that sometimes words can mean many different things. I did know that I wanted to hold the boy's hand.

Those art girls are definitely special. That's why they get a thousand likes when they post a photo. I get eighty on a good day, but I've been called special a thousand times. My dad thinks I'm special. Ivan thinks I'm special. Gideon thinks I'm special.

I think I'm special. That's why last night between texts with Gideon I Google "Do I have autism?" I know I don't even before I click through the two-minute quiz. If there is an interruption, I can switch back to what I was doing very quickly. I am good at social chitchat. When I was young, I used to enjoy playing games involving pretending with other children. I find making up stories easy. I do not find it difficult to imagine what it would be like to be someone else. I am not autisic, but there are questions that give me pause, questions I hit the AGREE button for. New situations make me anxious. I like to collect information about categories of things (e.g., types of cars, birds, trains, plants). When I talk on the phone, I'm not sure when it's my turn to speak. I tend to have very strong interests, then get upset if I can't pursue them. I tend to notice details that others do not. I know that I am not autistic—but I do have trouble existing in this world. I want to know why. I wish I could Google "Why am I the way I am?," "Is there a word for it?," "Are there other people like me?"

It seems like everyone is being diagnosed with autism these days. My generation has the most autists in history. If something is different, we have to name it. That's how language works. I want to matter and understand and know who I am and why I feel so strange. We young people hate binaries and love spectrums, but spectrums are vast and the scale scares us. This is why we live in the age of identity politics. This is why we need names. This is why we have asexuals and pansexuals and demisexuals. This is why we get even more specific with fraysexuals and quoisexuals and placiosexuals. This is why each of these identities has their own flag with their own colors. It feels so good to love a flag. To look at a pattern and know that it is yours. I only know two people who look at the American flag and feel like they belong. I get angry about identity politics. I read a little Marx so now I know that it is class that divides us and that capitalism will up and appropriate and commodify and then start using any words you use to define yourself to sell something to you. That doesn't mean that the words don't matter. Sometimes I laugh when I hear the words *demigirl* or *trigender* or *otherkin*, but other times I spend my evenings taking quizzes to see if I have autism. I understand the urge to belong, to have an identity with a name and know that out there, there are others like you. We all want to belong. We all want to be special.

Based

How do I begin to explain this word? By its opposite? There's Based and Redpilled and then there's its opposite, Cringe and Bluepilled. A "normie" won't know either of these terms. A "normie" might not even know what *normie* means.

When I say "cloud" I'm not referring to the things in the sky, unless that is where our data is kept. (Like how *avatar* was a Hindu deity and now it's a cyber identity, or how *wiki* used to just be the Hawaiian word for quick, or how a browser used to be a person who perused.) It's 2018 and I start saying "based," even while wondering if it will become the Gen Z equivalent of "groovy" or "cat's pajamas." I don't quite mean "to use [something specified] as the foundation or starting point for something." When I say "based," I'm not sure what I'm saying. Knowyourmeme.com, an online encyclopedia for all things new and cyber and in flux, does not separate the word *based* from the word *redpilled*: "Based and Red-pilled is a phrase that has been used on sites such as 4chan and Reddit to agree with and praise something, particularly something controversial. The opposite phrase is Cringe and Bluepilled." Unlike many encyclopedias, Knowyourmeme .com allows for comments. One commenter says, "This description is very unbased and bluepilled. Irony awareness levels 0." The idea that a dictionary or an encyclopedia can be edited and commented on is based.

Based does not have to mean right-wing, but it's often seen in reference to things that are red, things that disgust you. It's a way of saying "cool" or "I agree" in a language of a "right-wing" social group. But they do not own this language; nobody does. *Based* means different, and in our home-made cyber echo chambers, to lean toward the right has become an act of radicalism.

The American rapper Lil B or The BasedGod is the original source of the word *based*. Am I allowed to use etymology like that? No, but I'm going to anyway. There was a time when our whole generation laughed at the same jokes, listened to the same music, and loved the same rapper. Lil B was different from other celebrities. He followed everyone back, and if you sent him a selfie with his name written with Sharpie on your hand he would post it and you got to share a little of his fame. He replied to direct messages and retweeted fans and liked our selfies. This was radical, and it's how he very briefly transcended the classic limitations of celebrity. He was all-seeing and all-loving. He was like God. He had the power to really, truly create. True creation is the creation of something out of nothing that can become nothing again and anything in between. Humans and words are the only things I know that have this power. We both are born. We both can do good. We both can do evil. We both change. We both die. Do you think God stays in heaven because he too lives in fear of what he's created here on Earth? That's a quote from *Spy Kids 2*. We humans have run out of control, turned into something he didn't intend. This is what happened with The BasedGod's word.

Based was the term he used for his life and musical philosophy. Being based was a lifestyle that involved radical tolerance of others and revolt against societal rules and expectations. Shock was good and it was based. Currently, the top definition on Urban Dictionary is from 2009:

Based

Is when you dont care what people think
its a way of life

Doing what you want
how u want
wearing what u want

ex.

the LV book bag looks gay on you
idc im based

As we make up new words, they are added and sorted by how many votes they get. On the internet, time moves at hyperspeed, but Young Silence's words remain on top unchanged.

Young Silence's definition clarifies how this word that once meant something to someone has come to mean something else to someone else. It's a definition anyone can agree with, for a cool new word that of course we with our mushy young brains want to absorb and use. The definition comes from outside our time of echo chambers. It is here to remind us that the definitions of words are democratic. Language is a process that we are all part of. The walls of our echo chamber prisons keep us apart. They are built by algorithms, unseen hands, powers that be and will always be, but these walls are supported by us all and the words we choose to use. We have different ideas about stem cells and borders and guns, but that doesn't mean we need to start using different words.

Politics can create its own obscurantist language of alienating jargon, and for the sake of this country I think we should all be open to learning and sharing certain words, breaking down the walls letter by letter. *Based* belongs to whoever uses it, whoever chooses to define it, whoever chooses to follow the definitions that they see. We all have a little voice out here on the internet, in the classroom, over the telephone. We all have something to say. Remember that people can learn and learn best when they are not under attack or being talked down to. Remember that we all think different things are #BASED. Remember that this is what makes us little meaning-making, language-shaping, tweet-typing creatures, humans so #BASED.

Cringe

Cringe is the opposite of *based*, but a word cannot always be understood by its opposite. In fact, opposites are dead. Binaries are dead. There are inbetweens so vast one could fall into them forever and ever, growing old without hitting the ground. Hence, we need spectrums. Spectrums are bridges over the voids created by saying, this is not that. Girl is not the opposite of boy. Gay is not the opposite of straight. Black is not the opposite of white. Everything exists on a spectrum.

Spectrum is a word that elicits many responses. One of the most common is cringe. Spectrums are for the snowflakes with their identity politics and hurt feelings, for the left with the virtues they want you to know they have. That is why you will see it paired with the term *blue pill*.

A simple definition would be the feeling of disgust you get when something woke (see page 148) is too woke. The terms *fraysexual*, *quoisexual*, and *placiosexual* make me laugh. My friend Gideon explains that my laugh is not sincere. I'm not laughing with anyone. There is no joke except the one I am creating in my head. A more sincere response would be, cringe.

Like *based* and any of these new words I hear from Gideon, who is a true citizen of the internet, *cringe* is a word with an unstable meaning. One real, made-by-experts dictionary has two definitions for the word *cringe*. The first is "to bend one's head and body in fear or apprehension or in a servile manner" and the other is "to experience an inward shiver of embarrassment or disgust." The way I think about the cringe that I see on the internet is a mix of these two definitions. Fear, servitude, embarrassment, and disgust are all naturally interlinked. The idea of the spectrum is something that we are asked to accept and bow down to and never insult. To insult a spectrum makes one racist or sexist or homophobic or fascist or evil. A spectrum demands respect. It is worth respect, but the people who take it upon themselves to police this respect want people to bow down to not only the idea, but to the enforcers. This is what makes it cringe. Youth naturally find the idea that ideas are more powerful than questions to be cringe, as in cringing in fear and horror and disgust. We cringe because we are asked to accept something unconditionally. Unconditionality is a powerful and rare phenomenon. It can only be brought about through fear or love.

A common misconception about cringe is that it is commonly felt when something is too sincere. However, I would posit that it is quite the opposite. A cringe comes from the part of our mind that can detect danger. People using faux sincerity and sentimentality for political gain are a threat. We learn through feelings, but feelings can be forced into existence and the body knows this. Cringe is a response in our core, in the pit of your stomach. It is both a judgment and a fear, natural and created by the ideas we hold about how the world should be. I don't think cringe is like hate or leads to it. Hate is dangerous. Hate can arise when someone tries to make us not trust our instincts. Hate is something we rationalize and decide to feel. Cringe is in our lizard brains, at the base of our skulls. It's always been real, but now we are reminded, through its name, of its power. Next time you get the feeling, remember that it has a name, it doesn't have to curdle into hatred, and that it is okay.

Doomer

Do you feel so empty? Do you want to desire again? Are you a man? Are you in your mid-twenties? Do you stay up all night? Do you go on long walks? Did you grow up on the internet? Do you work a dead-end job? Do you listen to Radiohead? Are you haunted by the ghosts of futures that never happened? Do you know what *weltschmerz* means? Do you feel it? Do you feel too much? Do you feel too little? Do you hate? Do you drink? Do you smoke? Do you do drugs? Does it help?

Will anything ever help?

Does Schopenhauer help? Do you watch as the world falls apart? Do you care? Do you think a lot about nothing? Are you a product of these times? Have you ever felt at home on this earth? What have you inherited? Do you remember how to laugh? Do you remember how to cry? Are you doomed?

My boyfriend, Ivan, is a millennial. I don't think he knows the word *doomer*, but he says that my (best) friend Gideon is doomed. He tells me to watch out because doom is contagious and I was not vaccinated. Ivan is a Jew from Odessa, a refugee on paper, drowning in Ivy League loans and loving every minute of it. He believes that true struggle and immigrant parents made him immune to doom. He's thirty-three, lives in LA, and simply can't afford it. When he feels empty he makes movies. Doomers are stuck. They can't create and they can't consume. This is the source of the doom.

It's true that Gideon was a mess. He took lots of pills. He lived on benzos and beers. He felt nothing and everything and it filled him with fear. He withdrew from society and thesisized so hard. Then our government decided that he was worth a big fat grant and he decided that life was worth living. He withdrew from the pills and played basketball with the boys. He renounced critical theory for the summer and started to listen to Joe Rogan. He built a greenhouse with his hands. He makes minimum wage, but it is enough. Can you be doomed and then undoomed? Is doom permanent? Can you undoom yourself?

Doomers have swallowed the final pill. No, it's not the "red pill." The "red pill" wakes you up, or fills you with incel rage and makes you hate and post and post and hate. Doomers are post-rage, enlightened boys in basements with stubble on their chins and glassy eyes that cry no tears. They have accepted their loneliness. The doomers' pill is darker and more jagged, a catastrophic black capsule of apathy, denial, nihilism, fatalism, and defeatism. It might even be worse than those fake Xanax bars filled with fentanyl. It might be worse than OD'ing. When you OD it's over, just like that. When you're a doomer you're doomed for it to be over, over and over and over again.

A bloomer is someone who has escaped this cycle. They

are rare. They are older young men who saw some light and wanted to become the light. They are annoying and amazing, like a sunburn that turns into a tan. For example, they build stuff and plant stuff and create in the purest sense of creation with dirt and wood and seeds. It's not art, but what is?

Edgelord

Gideon and Ivan say starting my glossary with the word *autism* is a total edgelord move. An edgelord is a person who, according to Urban Dictionary, "uses shocking and nihilistic speech and opinions that they themselves may or may not actually believe to gain attention and come across as a more dangerous and unique person." An edgelord is a lover of both irony and sincerity. We/they live in the tiny space between these terms. Nothing feels real anymore (eerie). It's edgelords who embrace this. It feels so good to accept the instability of our times. It feels so natural, fun, and comforting to add to this instability. Perhaps this loving embrace is dangerous. When I think of edgelords, I remember that we members of this system will never be able to truly fight it.

When I met Gideon on that rainy spring night, under the blankets in my dorm, on my phone, in my Instagram DMs, I thought he was just a classic edgelord. But he made me laugh.

He made me uncomfortable and I love being uncomfortable. When I can pinpoint what is making me uneasy I feel less uneasy. When I am uncomfortable my thoughts race, and I love speed. Speed means my brain is working. A week after our internet encounter, he drove the two hours from him to me. We drank and we laughed and we thought. It was great and then it wasn't and then it was and now I don't know what it is.

Now it's summer and those kids are still in those cages and I care and my one really good friend does not. He reminds me that my caring and his not caring are actually the exact same thing. Neither of us is doing anything to help. He is being sincere. Maybe his edgy statement, this declaration of complexity, this act of edgelording, will drive me to take some sort of action.

I ask my mom to donate my frequent-flier miles to help lawyers get down to that border. I cry hot tears to Ivan and ask him to tell me that Gideon is wrong. He tells me that Gideon crossed the line a long time ago, that he is no longer an edgelord with an internship. Now he's a fascist with a government grant. Ivan tells me that he doesn't like Gideon, but that my hot tears are selfish and useless and Gideon is right about this. We are no different from him. Why should I cry about those kids and not the kids starving in Yemen or in refugee comas in Sweden? I tell my friend I care because it's my country and I paid taxes for the first time this spring. If you care about the kids, stop calling them those kids, he says. That's exactly the issue with edgelords, if you walk on that thin line you are bound to slip and cross over to one side at some point.

My mom tells me that caring is enough. I know that she's wrong. Caring is nothing. I sound like an edgelord when I say that, but I'm not trying to get a rise out of anyone. I'm just being honest.

Everyone calls Gideon an edgelord. He has a Fulbright, but he works at a construction site. He sends me a selfie in front of flowers he planted; he's wearing a T-shirt that says GOD BLESS AMERICA. I tell him it's a stupid T-shirt. He tells me it's not. I ask him if he's being ironic when he says that he loves America. He tells me that he is not an ironic person. The refugee children have to be kept somewhere. I tell him that they aren't allowed to touch each other, and that they are cold. He tells me that he wants proof, but doesn't care enough to get it himself. I ask him again if he's joking. He tells me that he's not. I'm mad, but I'm thankful that he is so honest. He is doomed and undoomed and doomed again, caught in a cycle of bloom and decay, between irony and sincerity. Is irony the enemy? Are edgelords the enemy? (Am I the enemy?)

There is no usefulness in the malicious provocation that people associate with the common definition of the term, but that's the great thing about our terrible times, everything is always changing, words are unstable, the term is no longer what it once was. It's something better, a word for complexity creators (cringe). It's something worse, a word for the wrong people who have crossed over into the dangerous right. To be completely transparent, it's something that I have been called many times. It's something people think that I am. In so doing, they have given me the job of actively defining the word in how I live and act and care. It feels good to have an identity. It's a big responsibility.

Fail

Epic fail. To mess up big time. Fail is to get hurt, to fall, to break, to destroy. Fail is an accident and it is so funny. It is always funny. On the internet, fail is written in impact font and ALL CAPS. **FAIL. FAIL. FAIL.** The font makes it funnier. It's the first meme I remember seeing. It's 2006 and I am in the school library. I'm on Google for the first time. I want to watch those videos of people falling and breaking things and slipping and accidentally punching each other. FAIL Compilations. When things go wrong, it's funny, that's what FAIL means. Failure is a universal humor, the simplest kind. It brings us together. We all can laugh because we can see how and why it went wrong. There is a right way and a wrong way.

That table is *obviously* not strong enough for all those people. The water in the pool is *obviously* frozen. The fence is *obviously* too high to jump. The mud is *obviously* slippery. You are obviously going to fall and we are all obviously going to laugh.

The fail meme is a meme of a bygone era, a long-ago time. A time when I could laugh with the crowd, when niche humor wasn't the only funny thing there was. A time before each of us who grew up on the internet filled our squishy, spongy brains with hyper-specific signifiers. When I try to explain a meme to my mom or dad, I fail. They haven't been loaded up with the signs and meanings that I have naturally mentally amassed since that day in the library in 2006. Other members of my generation have this same issue. We even make memes about this, our failure to understand anything but memes.

That fat Bugs Bunny is named Big Chungus. Do you even remember him? Should I remind you why he's funny? No. Does this failure to communicate across time make him funnier? Yes. When I'm saying something and you think I mean something else, is that funny? Sometimes. At the end of every year there is a meme that compiles all the top memes of the year by month. If I asked you to identify the memes in this image, would you fail? Yes. If I was asked to define *meme*, would it be an epic fail? Yes. Big Chungus, the image, is from 1940, so it's possible that Hitler saw him—and that's just the tip of the iceberg. Wikipedia says "An Internet meme, commonly known simply as a meme (/mi:m/, *MEEM*), is a cultural item (such as an idea, behavior, or style) that is spread via the Internet, often through social media platforms." A meme is democratic. Democracy makes it funny. When democracy fails, is that funny? I don't know. I know I laughed when Trump was elected. I laughed because I saw it coming, but knew it was wrong, like the slippery mud and the flimsy table and the pool with the frozen water. We should have seen it coming. Some of us deserved it. It was winter! Of course the pool was frozen. When we sat on the table we felt it wobble. The mud of the swamp is always slippery. Democracy didn't fail, we did, and it sure was epic. EPIC FAIL.

Ghost

A ghost is not a phantom, but a person who up and dropped out of your life, whose memory haunts you.

Gifted

Millennials, whom I don't identify with even though technically maybe I could, are always going on about how damaging it was to be told that they were all special, different, gifted. They'll be quick to tell you all about the drama and trauma of the gifted child, the fast pace of the internet's rise, the fact that they witnessed all that change faster than their little mushy brains could process it. They'll either tell you that no one is gifted, or that only they are, and that it was so, so hard. They were the first generation to all get trophies at sports games. The losers and the winners, no difference. Everyone was the same. High-five the other team. Eat those orange slices. Take off your cleats. Drink your Gatorade. Put your trophy on the shelf with all the other ones. It is a gift. Grow up. Wear ripped jeans. Try to be different. Try to be quirky. Wear glasses even if you don't need them. Be indie. That didn't work either. Everyone was indie, no one was independent. Sit in the basement, filled with doom. Blame the helicopter parents. Blame Urban Outfitters distressed denim. Blame capitalism. Blame the gifted program at your school. Blame the teachers for telling you how special you were. Blame the world for showing you it was not true.

Pausing to think about it, the whole idea of generations just plays into capitalism by encouraging new identities in order to exploit and divide us and sell us stuff.

Gideon and Ivan are both millennials. They both went to public school. They both lived in the type of suburb where there were only a few exceptional children, shining lights. Their second-grade teachers were right. Ivan is spiritually ahead of his generation. My generation was born knowing how special we were. We don't need to be different. We watch millennials as they try to be *individualist, entrepreneurial, politically correct, up on indie music,* and *hard at work on their personal brands.* We treasure our mumble rap. We laugh at some of their jokes, but most of their memes are weak. We Gen Zers are *collectivist, nihilistic,* and *interested in the playfulness of identity.* We know that nothing is stable, especially not the self. One minute you can be gifted, shining bright, in the front row, a National Merit Scholar, and the next you can be normal and sad and doomed and getting old, talking to me like your life depends on it. But these adjectives are all marketing. This is all just what they want us to think, to put a gulf between us.

Hyper

Hyperactive. Hyperloop. Hyperlink. Hypernormalization. Hyperbole. Hyperstition. Get Ritalin or Adderall or extra attention. Get from LA to San Francisco in a narrow tunnel. Get from here to there to everywhere with a click. Get born into a world shaped by narratives and lies. Get dramatic and make your own lies. Do it all very fast, faster than ever before. Do everything at hyperspeed because that's the speed your world moves at! Everything changes all the time. Be hyperaware of that. Don't hyperventilate. Welcome to your world. Everything here is hypercharged. You are hypermobile. You can do anything. So, do it the most! Do it to excess. Do it like you did when you ate refined sugar for the first time. Do it like you did it with frosting on your hands and face at your third birthday party. Do it like your mouth is filled with more Jolly Ranchers than teeth. They say you have attention deficit hyperactivity disorder (ADHD). But doesn't everyone? They say you're making stuff up, being hyperbolic. But isn't everyone? Everything is so very very. There is so much. It's so fast. Play *Mario Kart*. Play *Grand Theft Auto*. Steal your dad's Tesla. Accelerate. Match the speed you feel everyone else moving at. Stay with the pack. Read some Nick Land. Hate it. Love it. Take some Vyvanse. Zoom. Doom. Zoom. Doom. Zoom. At hyperspeed we click, click, click, six-second videos, learn, forget, run, binge, purge, do, do, do. We go so fast and do so much because we can see that the end is near. We want to see who can get there first. Are we there yet? Will we be the last? Will we get to see how it all ends? We're in a hypertunnel. Reality TV. Melting ice caps. Climate refugees. Automatic weapons. Mass extinction. The echoes of a vague shattering sound. We are so restless! We need to run. We run toward the light at the end of the narrow tunnel, even though we know that it's an oncoming train.

IRL

IRL=In Real Life. Define *in*. Define *real*. Define *life*.

When are we going to meet IRL? I asked this question to Gideon and Ivan, before they were hands and feet and blood, while they still lived behind the black glass of my screens. Before they were in my dorm or in a hotel room or in the flesh, they were already in my world. They were in my real life. They were men made of little pixels, of messages they typed and sent to me, but they were still real. When we met IRL, in person, face-to-face, it was strange. I didn't know your fingernails were like that. I didn't know about that freckle, that one right there. At first, those fingernails and freckles felt less real than what was behind the glass. IRL is always something different, always changing, just like everything else. What I am used to is what is real. Lately I am used to nothing.

People want to know if I meet all my friends on the internet. I don't! But I trust the algorithm just like I trust God. It's all been written. There's always a code to it. IRL or on the screen, it's all intelligent design. If you're reading this, future me, you're reading this because of the way those powers that be have programmed the world, with all their trends and policies and imaginings made real. Because of some process or set of rules that someone made and that we all follow. Algorithms are made not just of numbers but of words. There is no outside-of-online. Everything's real.

Joke

Everything is wrong. We just got here and the world is already ending. When things go wrong, we laugh. When things seem pretend, they're funny. When it turns out that it's real, it's even funnier.

Man goes to doctor. Says he's depressed. You've heard this one already. Says life is harsh and cruel. Says he feels all alone in a threatening world. Doctor says, "Treatment is simple. The great clown Pagliacci is in town tonight. Go see him. That should pick you up." Man bursts into tears. Says, "But doctor . . . I am Pagliacci." We are Pagliacci. We've taken the rainbow honk pill.

A fire broke out backstage in a theater. The clown came out to warn the public; they thought it was a joke and applauded. He repeated it; the acclaim was even greater. I think that's just how the world will come to an end: to general applause from an audience who believes it's a joke.

"Smile, because it confuses people. Smile, because it's easier than explaining what is killing you inside." Heath Ledger really got it. He got it before we got it. He told it to us as we sat spilling popcorn on our laps at our first hard PG-13 movie in 2008. We smile. It feels good to smile. Then there's the shooting in Aurora, Colorado, in a movie theater just like the one we sat in.

People die on the screen and off it, sometimes at the same time. The separation between spectacle and real life broke. It stayed broken. Nothing is IRL and everything is IRL. Reality is what we make it. It feels good to smile.

Ketamine

Super acid, special K, kitty valium, the big neigh. Ketamine is an anesthetic, but it feels like a psychedelic and it works like an antidepressant and it's the only party drug that provokes disassociation, so of course we like it. I heard it was for horses, but I put it up my nose anyways. Ketamine is what you imagined drugs felt like when you first heard about them. Coke is for millennials, for Patrick Bateman, for capitalists. Ketamine is for Gen Z and now it's legal and I have a prescription. The doctor says, imagine that depression is an infection. You are in pain. SSRIs are Advil. Ketamine is an antibiotic. As we get older, our brains get less mushy and spongy. Things get broken. Ketamine repairs them. Synapses or neurons or gray matter or something like that. It's the best drug. It's our drug. I do it off of Kevin's iPhone and on Maia's desk and in the bathroom in Berlin and at the clinic in LA. Life is harsh and cruel and smiling makes my cheeks hurt. Doom is contagious, but maybe we've found a vaccine. I wonder if it causes autism.

Lost

"You are all a lost generation," wrote Gertrude Stein, quoted by Ernest Hemingway in the epigraph for *The Sun Also Rises*. I'm in Paris by the river and I can't help but agree, although they weren't talking to us. The Lost Generation came of age during World War I. A lot of them were lost in the trenches. The rest were lost, as in "disoriented, wandering, directionless," in the streets and their lives. The older generations are worried about us, about 4chan and our smiling and our running with the pack. It's better to be lost, "disoriented, wandering, directionless," alone. There's a big problem when the whole pack is lost. They watched us grow up. They babysat and bullied us. Now we date them. They wonder if we are going to be the most conservative generation. They are worried about all this honking and rejecting the self. What do they know? They're doomed or bloomed. So what if we're a little lost and in this desperation to be found we've found each other and in each other found something horrible and delicious. Some of us voted for Hillary. Some of us voted for Trump. Some of us voted for Harambe, the dead gorilla. Do the trolls even know what they're doing or are they as lost as everyone else? Everyone is lost except for the bots. I don't know if I believe in horseshoe theory, but I do know that I believe in that tiny, but infinitely deep, space between irony and sincerity. Ironic voting is still voting and ironic hate is still hate. Within that deep, dark, tiny space is a huge void, where separate realities drift past each other like children's bubbles. Cheerful nihilism thrives. Come to think of it, I'm lost in that space. We all are. Gideon and I stand outside, sucking nicotine out of our little USB sticks. We can be lost forever, an abandoned satellite, Madeleine McCann, the Roanoke Colony, our baby teeth (yours and mine). No one knows where we are or where we are going. We are on the left and on the right, but we are all accelerating at the same rate. The faster it ends, the faster it can get better. Maybe we will reach a singularity. Full automation could be fun. Maybe we will see it end. Maybe we will see it start. Maybe we could have a war. A war with drones! A war just like the video games our older brothers play after school.

Me

Me! Me! Me! Me! A word impossible to define. A word that is fun to chant, but just like any chanted word the more you say it the less it means. A toy boat of a word. A word that demands distortion. Me. Me. Meme. That's a meme. An idea shared. Something transmitted, something that belongs to everyone. A meme is mine and yours. A fat Bugs Bunny, universal enough to make us all laugh. All the "me's" of our generation laughing at one thing. The self is so over. Let us all laugh together as one. Me. My first word. Not mama or papa. Me. Maybe it was just a baby sound, a test of the vocal cords, total nonsense, but I'm from LA.

Nerf

Nerf is a word that leaked off of a toy and into the video game world and back out into our Gen Z vocabs. I like it when words leak like that. We can squeeze and shape language and wash ourselves clean with it.

Nerf is an acronym, "non-expanding recreational foam." Neon toy guns. Automatics. Soft bullets. Lots of them. Blasters, not guns. Still automatic. The packages never say guns. You wouldn't buy your son a gun. Or would you? Who am I to assume? Running around with our socks on, jumping over the banister, hiding from the barrage of older brothers' gentle bullets. War in the playroom. That's what nerf is, but not what it means.

Older brothers and bigger boys took the word and used it in *Call of Duty*. *Nerf* is a verb now. *I'm gonna nerf all you faggots, give me that grenade.* It means to weaken or make less dangerous, usually in the context of weakening something in order to balance out a game, and is most commonly heard through headsets. Anyone can be nerfed, hit with those soft bullets, if someone decides they are a threat to the balance of our fragile game. When we nerf people IRL, we don't use foam bullets or digital bullets, sometimes we use real bullets, but mostly we use words.

A prevailing theory is that if we want to play fair, we should nerf rich white men. I guess that's sort of what #METOO is. A collective barrage of soft bullets against the wrinkled skin of the patriarchy, but I have my doubts. I don't know who should be weakened. I don't know how to restore balance to a game that has always been unfair. We're all implicated. To exist is to be a soldier in this war. Birth is conscription. We have all been training. What if I'm not ready? What if I can't fight? What if the big boys don't tell me what team I'm on? What if my socks slide on the hardwood floor? What if they find me hiding in the playroom? What if they laugh at me?

What if an orange foam bullet hits me in the eye, what then? Will I cry? Did I deserve it? Don't we all?

Oppressed

Being depressed is not the same thing as being oppressed. I am depressed, so I know what that word means. I have never been oppressed, so I struggle to define it. Depressed, I am down, in the ground, in the moist earth, in a hole I dug myself. Nobody put me here. I clawed at the earth with my own hands, like I was digging to China or a tunnel out of some death camp. I don't know why I wanted out or where I was trying to go. I don't know how long I spent digging, but I have been lying here cold and alone for quite some time.

If I was oppressed, there would be a shovel and someone holding the shovel and I would not be able to get out on my own. There would be others like me in holes near mine and others holding shovels keeping them down. The shovel holders would be benefiting from their actions. They would have some words to justify why they dug. Maybe it would be fun for them. Maybe they were convinced of some danger. Maybe they would just be following orders. Maybe it would be the way it was always done. That's the most terrifying possibility. The shovel holders might not even see the shovels in their hands. They might not even see the people they kept in the holes. They might go to school and work and vacation to the beach and eat spaghetti and have babies and struggles of their own, all while holding the shovels and keeping watch at the holes. Because that's the way it's always been done. Always is bad. Change is scary. Doom is not inevitable. Every now and again we should all check our hands for shovels. Chances are our hands are full and we have been digging for a long time. When you are at the beach or the Italian restaurant, look around and see who is not there. Even if you didn't dig the hole, there is a good chance you've walked by the empty lot where the holes are located. There's a good chance you didn't see them and didn't want to see them, even if you've spent years with your hands in the dirt digging your own hole, even if you've settled into that hole and feel comfortable there among the roots and worms.

To rise up and fight oppressive forces always takes a movement, a collective, a unified group. It should never be the job of the buried people to claw their way out alone. They have dirt in their mouths and eyes and still they have tried to get out. They spent years carving little tunnels between their adjacent holes and strategizing and rising and getting pushed right back down. They say you need a support system when you are depressed. That no one beats this disease, as they call it, alone, but depression is not oppression. It can be a by-product, but it is not the same thing. I put myself here and I will get myself out and I will try to help others. We cannot create a hierarchy of pain, but we have a hierarchy of needs at our disposal.

Like fireworks or electric scooters or huffing glue, irony can be fun, but also dangerous. If a joke isn't going to make someone pause and think and act and look at their hands for their shovel then maybe the joke isn't very funny? Even if it feels good and makes you feel smart and singular, like you get it. Most good jokes are ironic. All good things are dangerous.

I was born with a shovel in my hands, and I don't know what to do about it. I don't know if any of us do. Ivan and Gideon don't, but they are not women. When I hear a baby cry I hear it like it's my own child. I don't rush to help it, but I feel like I should. That's my lizard brain working. Back in the caves, when survival was even harder, we took better care of children we did not birth. That communal care is why we survived the ice ages and the saber-toothed tigers and the Crusades. Maybe once the ozone melts it will come in handy again. I tried to make Ivan and Gideon listen to the recording of the kids detained at the border crying for their parents, but they didn't want to hear it. I know that even if they had heard it, it wouldn't have meant much to them. Gideon says he wants to have a baby. Maybe once he does he will feel differently about the cries of children whose faces he's never seen. Maybe then he could put his face he gave his child onto one of those screams. Maybe then we would do something. Ivan says the recording wouldn't mean much to him because he knows there are children crying, touch-starved, cold everywhere in the world and they have always been crying and they always will be. I know that he wouldn't say this, that he doesn't identify with the label on his immigration papers, but the kids on the recording are like him. He was once one of the children, hungry and scared, but he was in his mother's arms and that made all the difference. His shovel is not as strong as mine. He is less complicit, but I don't think there's a point in making some hierarchy of complicity. It's a spectrum, but there is no point in breaking it down with words, demicomplicit, transcomplicit, bicomplicit. We all live in the same cave. There is a danger. Children are crying and most of us don't care, or do care but don't act. We should all feel complicit. We should all care. I don't know why caring comes so naturally, yet I have never taken any action.

Do I not care enough? Do I care because caring feels good and I want to feel good? Do I care because the tears I cry make me virtuous? Do I want people to see my tears? Are my tears my only action? Is this inability to act *doom*? Yes. I think it is. They were right, doom is contagious. My doom has spread down to the border and keeps those children cold in their metallic blankets. I cry. What other action is there to take? What does it mean to drop your shovel? I don't know much, but I do know that no one should be trapped in a hole alone. No one should be buried in an unmarked grave. No one should have their children taken from them. No one wants a Holocaust comparison, but isn't this what we learned on those field trips we all had to take to museums of tolerance? Maybe all I have written, this flowery extended metaphor about holes and dirt, is a mere exercise of my privilege, a little fancy dig of my shovel. Writing about other people's oppression is an exercise that ultimately may have removed some weight from my own shoulders, some dirt from my chest. It has nothing for anyone who needs it. Gideon would say if you have time to write down a glossary, you do not need help digging yourself out and just want to feel better. Gideon wants to feel better, but he would never profit directly from other people's struggle. That is reprehensible. I may as well have written this with the tip of my shovel on newly packed earth.

Pill

Red pill. Blue pill. One pill. Two pill. Mad pill. Sad pill. Pills are ideas that change our body chemistry, the way our brains work, everything about us. We take them when we are in pain. They make us feel better in their absoluteness. They make us feel worse in the long run. On the internet, in a world-class example of semantic shift, there is a new type of pill. They are idea pills and just as dangerous as real pills.

Here's what they say. Red pill makes you uncontrollably angry and entitled. Green pill fills you with conspiracy theories. Black pill dooms you. Honk pill makes you laugh at it all. A choice in Morpheus's hands. Wake up and see how far the rabbit hole goes, or go back to how it was. Wake up. Be woke. Once a pill works there is no going back. That is that. Your body and brain are chemically changed. We are always already bluepilled, per the incels. Blue pill is what we get in our vaccines, and vaccines are mandatory. Red pill is a choice and a hard one, again per the incels: the choice to see the world how it really is, a place where women play you and Jews control you and you should be in control. The promise of being awake is alluring. Lots of young men take it. When they take it they awake in a new world, but that new world is a construction, even more of a construction than the old one. It's a new world with a single and totalizing narrative. It's the world we must make sure this one does not become.

This winter, I was honestly afraid I was getting redpilled. I began to hate phrases like *safe space* and the idea of identity politics and infantilization. It felt like I was being infected by some awful disease, so I took a bunch of (blue) Adderall and read a bunch of books as fast as I possibly could. Reading is not like a pill. Ideas on each page can be snacked upon and digested, at whatever speed your body works. It's healthier that way. Most things are healthier if they are done slowly. A pill is one fast thing, one color, a totalizing idea. Books are the opposite, full of so much, rainbowy.

I go to the ketamine clinic because I like to feel. I want to feel, but I don't want to feel like I'm:

- Alone in this threatening world anymore

- Being hunted for sport

- A character being written by a man

- The crazier one

- The less crazy one

- Misunderstood

- Only real when I'm talking to Ivan or Gideon

- Searching for actors for my life's open roles

I want to know that there are others like me. I want to meet them IRL. I'm anti-pill. I'm straight edge. I'd rather cut myself than do Xanax. No, I'd rather cut myself then do Xanax. I want to calm myself through feeling and unfeeling. I want a pill for that.

I wonder what would have happened if Neo grabbed both of the pills in Morpheus's open hands and stuffed them both down his throat. Would he have ended up like me? Stuck in the middle and loving it and hating it and loving it?

Quirk

We all have quirks, those little things that make us endearing, those tiny trivial differences that make us matter. Gideon and I could be exactly alike. The world probably doesn't need us both, but maybe someone in this world needs to see the way he sucks off all the meat of a peach pit and keeps it in his mouth so gently and for so long like a precious stone that needs smuggling or a robin egg that needs incubating. We are all eccentrics. It's 2018 and there is no other way to be. Being weird isn't weird anymore. Quirky is cool is quirky is cool. Until it is not, and you have a tattoo of a mustache on your finger and the bangs you cut weirdly short will not grow out right.

Key and historic quirks, -cores, aesthetics:

- Vaporwave

- Health Goth

- Seapunk

- Coquette

- Tomato girl microaesthetic

Quirky reached its peak when I was in seventh grade. Everything I thought was cool could be found at the same store, and if it wasn't there this week it would be the next. Manufacturing speeds accelerated and matched the growth and emergence of trends. But millennials fought back. Individuality felt like their God-given consolation prize, their post-soccer-game orange slice time, a part of life that could not be erased, but it was. There was *New Girl* and *Moonrise Kingdom* and pop-punk. Trends went viral. Nothing belonged to anyone. Individuality was stripped of its rite of passage status. The only forms of revolt were a complete rejection of quirk, normcore—"an anti-aspirational attitude, a capitalization of the possibility of misinterpretation"—or an embrace of trends, signifiers, and clothing that were too controversial or aesthetically unappealing to be mass-produced. Eventually these forms of revolt became quirks themselves and the quirks ended up at Urban Outfitters, near the Ramones T-shirts and the ripped sweaters.

If ugly can become beautiful and the 90s have been cool since the 90s and girls born in the year 2000 dress just like the pop stars who topped the charts on the day they popped out, then nothing will ever be able to go anywhere. If we exist within boundaries, we cannot push them. That is why certain members of Gen Z have embraced them on Musical.ly. They all lip-synch to whatever song is trending and perform identical little rituals and dances to go along, to not be alone. This is why other members spend hours in chat rooms looking for the group that best matches their niche ideology: feminist libertarians, monarchists, queer ecosocialists, young Hegelians, transfascists. As Gen Z comes of age, we find the packs within the packs. An embrace of the pack, a drive to follow and fit in, to let go of our fetishization of quirk is new. We have come so far that the act of fitting in becomes the most rebellious thing one can do. I wonder where the girls with mustache finger tattoos are now.

Rage

Rage seems to be the most important emotion of our times. Everyone is angry. *If you're not angry you're not paying attention!* It doesn't matter whom you are angry at, you should be angry at someone. Rage is an energy, like wind in a turbine or sun on a panel or water in a wheel. If we can harness it, then maybe we can save ourselves.

Aren't you angry? we get asked. *We left you a dying earth. Shouldn't you be doing something about it? Shouldn't you at least be mad?* I don't think that I've ever felt rage.

Once, Gideon punched a wall until his knuckles bled. He laughed when I told him he was just angry because he didn't get what he wanted. He laughed and asked me if there was any other reason to be angry at all. Rage stems from entitlement, and entitlement is not always something to be ashamed of. We are all entitled to safety and justice (whatever that means?) and probably a lot more. When these needs are not met, when they are stolen or withheld, rage seems like a very proper response. Rage seems like a means of survival. Punching a wall seems like a fine enough use of rage. It won't save you, but it helps. Maybe one day we can get all the angry young men together who feel like something that should be theirs, always was theirs, is being taken from them. We could set them up in a field with a huge wall and they could punch it all day long and we could harvest the strength of their punches and power a town for a night or two. It wouldn't have to be a small town. I'm sure we would have many wall-punching men driving in from across the state, to be a part of something that mattered, to use their anger for something real. If I could send them all to fight with the enemy for a year I would. I think it would be good for their rage. Their natural and primal male rage, not a symptom of toxic masculinity, just a symptom of being a man with thousands of years of knowledge on how to conquer, protect, kill, define, destroy, avenge, maim, make, smash, fix, pillage, and build buried deep at the back of their skulls. Sometimes I feel a twinge of rage, a surge of denied entitlement when I remember that I do not possess this same ancient knowledge, even though it is something I feel I deserve. The idea that I feel like I deserve something gives me another tiny twinge of what might be the first symptoms of rage.

Safe

A safe place used to be a place where you were not going to get hurt. Now a safe place is a place where you are not going to feel hurt. Feelings became facts at some point between 2016 and now. When boys are gentle I am always surprised. When the members of a space decide to call it safe they should be thanked. Everyone should be kept safe; most of us already are. The people who came before us left a dying planet, but they have decided to provide us with some safe spaces. Thank God. In these spaces I will not feel hurt. When the fires come, I know where I will be, right by the self-care station with the mandalas and the chai.

Tender

To be tender, to be vulnerable, to be understanding, to be good. Jenny Holzer put letters up on a movie marquee: "It is in your self-interest to find a way to be very tender." Gen Z girls and gays take these words and make them the words underneath their names on Twitter and Instagram. Everyone wants to be tender. Smol beans, soft bois, tender queers, delicate flowers, a/sexual aesthetic, shy, dressed in pastel primary colors, murmuring "henlo nice 2 meet u." Why? Tender things must be protected. We all are afraid. The world is scary. Health insurance is expiring. Maybe if we are tender, someone will protect us.

Did Jenny Holzer mean that we ourselves should be soft or that we should be gentle with others or that these things go hand in hand and those hands are called tenderness? Those are hands we should all hold. We all deserve safe spaces, places to go and be held and color in mandalas if that helps. We all must create these safe spaces in our own lives for others. We don't need meditative coloring books. All we need is tenderness. How hard can that be? Probably very soft.

Troll

- The first one was a trans internet user of Stewart Brand's The WELL with the log-in name "Grandma"; all other trolls followed him.

- Lives under bridges among the tall green grass, wearing rags, preying on travelers and innocent bearded goats.

- Became a verb

- In cute times, 4chan trolled a poll to send Pitbull to Alaska; in less cute times, 4chan trolled a poll to send Taylor Swift to a school for the deaf; in strange times, 4chan found Shia LaBeouf's art project flag from its livestream's constellations and contrails and replaced it with a Trump hat (or did he pay them off, was it a lie all along?); in scary times, 4chan is constantly filled and refilled with rape threats, ghosts, neighborhood graffiti, dark triad traits and behaviors, anime characters with souls, and twisted extremism.

- *Troll* is one of many magic- or fairy-tale-coded words floating through the internet, along with *ghost*, *avatar*, *cursed*, *main character*, and *frog*. Trolls used to live in isolation under bridges, to be avoided by travelers, but now they live in basements and penthouses and suburban duplexes. A mythological troll is ugly and dirty and lives in a dark place, and its magic is dwarfed by that of its digital namesakes. Trolling (the practice, in cute times) takes one back to a childlike sense of wonder.

UwU

This isn't a word. It's an emoticon. It's a feeling. It's the face you type when "omg" or "awwwww" is not enough to convey how cute, how warm, how soft, how tender, how pure, how wholesome something is. U is an eye. W is a mouth. U is another eye. UwU is you. UwU is a string of letters that means something, the same thing to everyone who has seen it before. Doesn't that mean it's a word? How is it pronounced? If it is a word, what language is it in? Is it part of a language in a fetal stage, WuwWuwism? Something being built right before our eyes? Can we add new words to this language? Or is that just dumb as fuck?

It's a new word, from an unborn language, but it already has a history and a connotation other than its original meaning. It's unfortunately seen as creepy or cringe. The word men use when trying to appeal to teenage girls. There are entire blogs dedicated to documenting "UwU Culture," as they call it. Every year since 2015, it has been collectively redefined. Cute. Creepy. Cringe. Cringe (furry). Always in flux, just the way language has always been, but now with hyperlinks.

Virtue

Virtue, the word, has had a rough go of it lately. It sets off sensors in the center of the deepest and oldest parts of the brain. Virtue. We have said it too much, like when we were little and we said "toy boat, toy boat, toy boat, toy boat, toy boat, toy boat, toyboat, toyboat, toyboat, toboayt, tobayat, toabyat." Virtue is nothing but a tongue twister, a game, a competition. Who has the most? Who can show it off the best? Who is watching my virtue? Whose virtue am I watching?

Virtue signaling, as we know it in our digital and academic Gen Z circles, is the practice of showing you care, but without putting in any other work. I care, and I want you to know that I care, because maybe that will make you care about me. After every school shooting a post, #NEVERAGAIN. All black is worn to award shows. #NEVERAGAIN. Long paragraphs denounce rapists we've never met. A callout. Special filters on profile photos, flags of the country attacked. Loud sparkly signs. #NEVERAGAIN. As a whole, us zoomers hold such signaling in disdain, but within each is a kernel of hope. A sincere little piece of hope. A hope that it never happens again, but then of course there is an again and another again and another. A hope that somehow, something you post matters. A hope that someone cares about you. I hope that you matter.

In a few isolated churches across our nation, mostly Pentecostals, Charismatics, and other evangelicals, there still exists a tradition of snake handling. This ritual consists of holding venomous snakes and not being bitten, in order to show the other churchgoers your piety. A gentle snake is a signal of your virtue. Hundreds have died.

I wonder if we'd have as much virtue signaling as we do if posts could bite. Is the reward worth the risk? Are you pure? Do you matter? Is anyone ready to really hold the snake?

Woke

If you took the red pill you have woken up, but that's a very different type of woke. The red pill is for the right and woke is for the left or maybe it's the same type of awake, the type of alertness that hurts. Maybe everything has always been the same, just circles and spirals and mirrors. Sometimes being awake is painful and all you want to do is curl up in some safe space with someone's or no one's arms around you. When we wake up and see the world differently, start to recognize power structures, see the algorithms set up, realize our own part in it all, how do we know that we are all waking up in the same reality anymore? I live in clown world. I've touched both of Morpheus's hands. I feel safe all the time. Maybe you wake up somewhere else. When I first heard the word *woke*, I was fifteen and on social justice Twitter. Now I hear anti-semitic New World Order conspiracy theorists using it, but it means the same thing.

I shouldn't try to speak for my generation; this is just a

preliminary glossary, some words of interest, some words that have defined us and some words we have defined.

X

Every word here was once written somewhere else for the very first time, cross-bred or loaned or imagined from nothing. Right now I'm probably living before some word you can't imagine your life without. I'd like to shout out John Milton, the English language's most prolific neologizer and creator of more than six hundred words (including the hits *lovelorn*, *pandemonium*, and *irresponsible*), and to quickly note the nine most common ways words are created:

- **Acronym:** *Laser* stands for "Light Amplification by Stimulated Emission of Radiation," but on the other hand, *taser* stands for "Tom A. Swift Electric Rifle" because Tom A. Swift was the protagonist of the inventor's favorite childhood book series.

- **Affixation:** Adding established prefixes or suffixes to existing words, ex. *hyper+reality=hyperreality*. *OED*'s earliest known use of the word is from around 1970. Before that I guess reality felt more real and the word was not needed.

- **Back-formation:** Creating a new word by removing an affix from an existing word. For example, *edit* was created perfectly by removing the *-or* from *editor*.

- **Borrowing:** *Neologism* itself is a loanword from French, borrowed in the late 1700s and never changed again.

- **Coinage:** Inventing completely new words with little to no historical connection to existing words, no process but that of the imagination, just vibes. Coined words are often born with copyrights, but a well-coined word will escape the chains of intellectual property through genericization, the natural open sourcing of language: *escalator, kerosene, google, jacuzzi, velcro, rollerblade.*

- **Compounding:** When a word combines two complete words. There's the mundane *toothpaste, teaspoon, bathtub.* There's the less obvious but still unsurprising *anybody, online, yourself.* There's the sublime metaphorical sweetness of *rainbow, wishbone, keepsake, cupcake, butterfly, skyscraper.* Imagine being the first person who ever said *butterfly* or the guy who decided the building would scrape the sky. And then there are some so logical that they are lovely or so lovely that they are logical, the ones compounded in perfect flow. Words we forget could have ever been apart, like: *no-thing, no-body*; words we forget where to even split in two, *no-where/now-where/now-here.*

- **Portmanteau:** *Brunch, incel, edgelord, spam, goon, chocoholic, smog, himbo, chortle, snark, goldendoodle,* and I could go on forever.

- **Reduplication:** This word formation process, referring to semi-repeating a word within itself, feels whimsical, like baby talk. Sometimes it means a word gets repeated to signify its smaller than usual size, *chitchat, pitter-patter, splish-splash.* In other languages, reduplication changes definitions, but in English, it's just for fun.

- **Semantic change:** One of our more mystical linguistic creation processes, in which a word is imbued with a new definition but unchanged visually. It remains identical on the page and to the ear yet different in the brain, real-life alchemy. Once the literal becomes figurative, even just once, the whole word can begin to drift away from its meaning and into something new. Unlike the other linguistic neologism creation processes, this can take lifetimes. Yet it seems that sometimes these shifts and drifts from the real to the figurative and then from that figurative into our new real follow some sort of logical magic or magical logic, an imperceptibly constant motion, like the earth spinning around and around or gravity or God. The word *silly* started off meaning blessed, back in its Old English pre-shift definition. Then the meaning shifted from blessed into innocent through the Middle Ages' generations of speakers, and then it became what it is. That is, you are blessed to be innocent and then you are naïve because of your innocence and finally your naïveté makes you a fool.

Young

There's a meme that goes, would you rather go crazy or go stupid? I don't know why it always makes me laugh. Maybe I laugh just because I don't know why. The mystery of it gets me. Being young is having a million questions while loving a mystery that will never be solved. Being young is feeling like the end is near. We have climate change. They had nuclear war. Everyone had something. For as long as we stretch forward there will always be something. Being young is going crazy and going stupid all at once. Being young is about extremes and Gen Z is so young and so extreme. Desperate times call for desperate measures. All times are desperate. Desperation is part of being human. I'm desperate to define myself and redefine myself because that is what it means to be young. Remembering that you won't be young forever is hard when you have been young forever.

Zoomer

We are called Generation Z. *Z* is the last letter of the alphabet, but we will not be the last generation. It feels like that sometimes, but feelings are not always facts and some of us Gen Zers have babies of our own. They don't have a name yet, but we will probably call them Generation Alpha. They are not the beginning. They are a beginning, just like we were. We are zoomers. We are speeding toward something. The earth spins so fast. Sometimes it goes so fast that I want to get off, but most of the time I am thankful for the speed.

I am a zoomer and we were, after all, built for this. I wonder if we will ever get to where we are going. I wonder how much will change before it's all over. We are zooming into the future where everything matters, where we matter, where what we do together matters. Being young is so cool. We are crazy and stupid and full of ideas. Everyone who has been young knows this. I'm sure you remember being filled with this brief and powerful and perfect feeling. The feeling that you and your friends and everyone your age are the most important people in the world. I am so spoiled and lucky and safe, and every wish I've ever made has come true at least a tiny bit, well maybe not the pony, not world peace, not now that I've said them out loud.

We are the future of the planet, held together by the same

meme signifiers and memories of school shootings, united by how spongy our brains were when those big things happened. I don't think the hyperpolarized members of my generation will magically come together and collectively accelerate us into some full automation utopia. I don't know what we will destroy together, the national parks we will pillage, the deserts we will invade, the animals that will die out under our care, what will happen when those resources run out, whose children we will put in cages.

We are what we have been called and diagnosed with and what we write in our bios. Identity is a Swedish prison, comfortable but still you can't leave. The floors are made of that IKEA wood; we cannot use a spoon to escape. Feelings are not facts unless we decide that they are. We can escape by creating. Time has never moved faster than it is moving right now. We are not doomed as long as we keep going. We are algorithmically and tenderly filled with life and vaccines and nicotine vapor. We are the products of our time and soon our time will be a product of us. Isn't that terrible? Isn't that wonderful? I can imagine a world where the same word means both. We already have our own language.

written by sad girl in the third person

```
¯(__(_____(_____¯_0
            __         🔥
           |  |      {*}
           |  |    __V__
           |_|o_|⊛⊛⊛|0_
             |          |
             |    ♡     |
             |_____|
```

round 3 a.m. she opens her parents' bedroom door and watches them sleep. She wants to ask them who she is. She spends her nights wondering about that while smoking cigarettes on the roof and eating Tums like candy. They made her, so they should know the answer, but she knows they don't. They're as clueless as she is, as clueless as babies, so she pretends that they are hers. She at once wants to have a baby and to be a baby. These two desires are ruining her life. She tells herself that her life is something real enough to be ruined, but deep down she knows that not enough has been built to be destroyed. This isn't a comforting thought. Her life, her real life, her adult life is beginning. She is twenty-two now and there are no more comforting thoughts to be had. Maybe that is what adulthood is all about. Maybe she can find some comfort in that.

She loves her boyfriend, but he isn't her baby and she isn't his. He holds her and she feeds him. He protects and provides and she amuses and cleans. He teaches her things and she teaches him other things. They play games and laugh and cry together. Sometimes she feels like his baby. Other times she feels like he is hers. It's not enough, she tells him.

Her boyfriend jokes that "want" is her favorite word. She is always asking for things, always trying to fill some void. She wants a cigarette or an agent or satin pillowcases or peace in the Middle East or AirPods or to understand how the CIA works or to have sex or to not have sex or to be skinny or to be pregnant or to be no one or to be someone. She knows that the end of desire will be the end of all suffering. She knows how to meditate. She knows she can stop wanting, because she does not need and want comes from need. She has never had to need. She's always been somebody's baby. Maybe that is why she feels the need to have her own. Maybe wanting a baby and wanting to be a baby are what womanhood is all about. Maybe she can find some comfort in that?

She makes a long list of ways that babies are like books and books are like babies. They both are time-consuming. They both can be carried. They both bring comfort. They both smell good. They both can be thrown across a room. They both belong to someone. They both can be burnt. They are both useless. They are both beautiful. They both can belong to her. There are already so many of them on earth. She can make more. Almost anyone can write one or have one. Almost everyone should. They both can change the world. They both can amount to nothing. If she made a book or a baby it could tell her who she is or maybe make her into something new and knowable, just as she made it. She wants to know herself. She wants to know what matters. She wants to hold and be held. She wants to push something out of herself and into a separate existence. She wants to be loved and to love and to be loved and to love. She wants to stop wondering who she really is.

She's a white, upper-middle-class Virgo zoomer who celebrates both Hanukkah and Christmas. She is the only child of Gen X coastal elite hipster atheists who own their home, lease their car, and hate it all. She is godless. She has been diagnosed as bipolar II, but she is not that. She has been diagnosed with clinical depression and obsessive-compulsive disorder. She has these mental illnesses and she has a vagina and she mostly uses it for sex with people with penises who identify as men. She laughs when she reads *mental illnesses* and *people with penises who identify as men.* She's privileged enough to laugh. That is who she is. She is sad. That is what she knows, but the knowable is not enough. She hates when people announce that they hate labels. She hates labels. She doesn't like to look at flags. She likes to think that she would never call herself bisexual or Jewish, but she often does in a sort of roundabout way. She thinks identity politics are mostly a bad idea. She can explain her stance some other time.

She will quote Žižek and Marx and Houellebecq and whoever else is trendy and probably call something retarded. She will not identify her beliefs as post-leftism, but that is what they are technically called and if she believes them it means that is what she is, a post-leftist with a nicotine addiction and a vagina and white privilege and obsessive-compulsive disorder and a birthday in September. She's a registered Democrat, but she doesn't like registering for anything or voting for most people. Why would she want to join any club that would have her for a member? She likes to smoke. That must mean that she is a smoker. She likes to write. That can't mean that she is a writer. She wants to make her life out of writing. She does not want to tell people that she is a writer. She doesn't know what a writer is. If you make a baby, are you a mother? If you make a book, are you a writer? If you want to make a baby, you are not a mother. If you want to make a book, you are already a writer?

If you tell people you are something, that is what you are. If you tell people you do something, that is what they think you are. She smokes, so she is a smoker; she writes, but she is not a writer. She knows that what one does is not necessarily who they are. She knows that action-based identity is one of the greatest tricks neoliberalism ever pulled. She knows that's the sort of thing you can write in a personal essay, and that the personal is probably political. She doesn't know quite how confused she sounds. But she knows she is anti-neoliberal, and she knows she thinks she knows what that means. She knows that capitalism is evil. She doesn't yet know how wrong she is. She knows evil is a silly word. She has never been called evil, to her face.

She hates telling people who or what she is. She knows this hate must come from some incredible place of privilege, the privilege to live without pride, the privilege to have nothing precarious enough to protect yet, the privilege of being normal.

She will never be Joan Didion; she doesn't quite know that yet. She knows that she's not enough. Sometimes, late at night, she smokes cigarettes and hopes that something bad will happen to her so she can write a good personal essay.

She believes that one day she will quit smoking and she will be an ex-smoker and that one day she will be able to explain her beliefs to her children if they ask. Maybe she's wrong. Maybe that is what she is, wrong and white and middle class and a smoker and childless and writing a personal essay. Maybe she's something else. Maybe someone can unpack it for her. Maybe she needs to be called out or canceled or educated or told to educate herself. If you ask, she will tell you that she is lucky. She feels young and lucky and addicted to cigarettes, the way she imagines some people feel female or communist or Canadian. Sometimes when it's time to announce names and pronouns, she wants to say nobody and nothing. Don't refer to her as anything. She's not even really here.

In the grand scheme of things, most people are never really even here. They're born and they're here and then they're dead and they're gone and then everyone who remembered them is dead too. Most books don't get a second printing. The big ideas stick around, but who decides what the big ideas are and who keeps them safe? She wonders if that is her role, some protector of ideas, keeping memories safe until it's time for them to be passed on. This idea frightens her. The world is scary. It's just the way things are. The past gets bigger and the future shrinks. No matter who she becomes, she will stay the exact same size, but soon she will know who she is. Or at least she will know who she's not. Too bad she just missed the personal essay boom.

To make herself feel like someone, she could build a hyper-specific identity, or brand herself like a cow or a vlogger. Instead she writes personal essays. She is not special. She knows that. She is here just like everyone else, trying to make something that will last longer than their corporeal form, whether it matters or not. She's here to be a baby and to have a baby. To hold and to be held. To arrive and to leave something behind on departure, even if that something is just a yummy snack for a worm.

She thinks about mass graves in Central Park and imagines everyone she's ever known, all the skater thems, literary magazine editors, Catholic cokeheads, bodega cats, hype-beasts, and personal essayists curled up together under the dirt, a real feast for the worms. She thinks about how who they thought they were won't matter, because it never really did. All that matters is what's left behind.

She wants to wake up her parents and ask what they have made besides her, but she lets them sleep because she already knows what they will say. They will tell her that she is the greatest thing that they ever made. She will know that she is not all that great, but compared to the money and those good investments and her mom's crochet animals and her dad's straight-to-video movies, it's true, she is the greatest thing her parents ever made. If she woke them up, they'd ask why she smells like cigarettes and if she wants to get lung cancer and if she thinks she's invincible or that smoking makes her interesting. She would tell them that, like them, she is dust and she will return to dust. The question is what will remain.

At the Party

```
    _      _      _      _      _
  __( )__( )__( )__( )__( )__
'--.  .--.  .--.  .--.  .--.  .--'
 /  _  \/  _  \/  _  \/  _  \/  _  \
(/  \) (/  \) (/  \) (/  \) (/  \)
```

At the party, someone tells someone that they heard that I make rape jokes. I ask someone who told them that and they tell me that it was someone else.

"Yeah," someone else tells me, "I heard you make rape jokes."

"Where? Where'd you hear that?"

"Around."

"Damn okay," I say. Someone else laughs. "I'm gonna rape you," I say. I say it again, this time louder, "I'm gonna rape you." Someone else stops laughing. It's a joke. Get it? A rape joke, because I make rape jokes.

At the party, someone is upset and no one is laughing. "I've probably been raped as many times as they've told a good joke," I say. Now everyone knows.

Somebody says, "That's the first rape joke I've heard you tell."

"Well, it won't be the last." This is my thing now. "Hey, everyone, what's worse than a rape? A rape joke."

"Heard that one before." Yeah, that one wasn't very clever. Someone says that I'm canceled and everybody says that I'm drunk or coked-up or stupid. Somebody says that I'm "drunk and coked-up and stupid and, also, canceled." I'm "Baa"-ing or bleating or whatever in everybody's faces, explaining, "Hey, I'm trying to speak your sheep language!" I'm laughing and "Baa"-ing. Totally out of control. Who can blame me? Everyone laughs. No one is actually offended.

After my rape jokes, someone squirts me with a water gun. "Canceled," they say.

"I hope you're reincarnated as a foie gras goose," I say.

"Jesus, that's harsh," somebody says. It's just a joke. Now someone is shooting everyone with a squirt gun! Everybody is screaming and wet and no one knows what's real anymore. Everybody is out of control and I am everybody.

"This is like Columbine!"

Somebody says that no, it's not like Columbine. I guess it's not.

At the party, I'm dancing with someone or maybe just near someone. I'm all alone, really, and I'm yelling. "Do you know who I am?" Do you know who I am? Do you know who I am?

Somebody probably thinks I mean that I think that I am somebody or that I will be somebody, and/or that I mean that they are nobody and will stay nobody. That's not what I mean. I'm not that mean. I'm yelling because I don't know the answer. Do you know who I am? Do you know who I am? Can anybody tell me?

The End

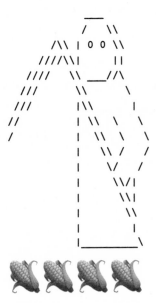

Her hair had already begun to fall out by the time the Mormon supersoldier came down from the mountain. Began or begun, she wasn't too sure which. There was no way to check anymore. No one to ask. No one to tell. It didn't matter. Nothing much did by then.

Stuff used to matter. Stuff used to matter every day. Stuff used to matter so much that they'd write stories about it. She could remember that. She could remember stories and something called bedtime, being under the blankets, chewing on the shiny cardboard of anti-racist baby books, and playing on the tablet, sticky fingers on the screen, hot November days of snow cones and talking to talking baby dolls. She could remember being very small not too long ago, and wars within wars, and 4D infographics about population control, and the ouch of the insertion of a birth control implant under her arm, and being in a boy's arms under the abandoned ski lift, and starless skies and kisses and screenshots of screenshots, and her name and parts of the national anthem, but she didn't. She didn't remember any of that by the time the

Mormon supersoldier handed her a can of corn and began his mask-muffled prayer.

Even if she could hear what he was saying, it wouldn't have made any sense, since sense itself had long since come to an end. Lots of ends had come and gone, long before the girl or the Mormon supersoldier had even begun to begin. This particular end had been beginning and beginning and beginning. People looked for it on the horizon at the break of each new day and in the headlines as news broke each day. The universe seemed to be shrinking, but of course it was not. It had been like that for centuries: The seams are ripping, it's all falling apart, unprecedented, unprecedented, reality is ending, the country is dangerously polarized, democracy is dying, the polar bears are dying, fascism is rising, history is ending, the sea is rising, history has ended, our story is over, it's all your fault, it's not your fault at all, you don't even matter. It was this terrible sort of end, generations and generations old, that no one could know or see the whole of, but everyone felt it, since they had been born and lived whole lives under its long, looming shadow, a slow, slouching spiral widening and widening. People repeated and repeated, *Things fall apart, the center cannot hold, haven't you heard, things fall apart, the center really cannot hold*. They said it so many times and in so many different words that it became a prayer in reverse. When the day came, it meant nothing at all and no one was ready, except a few Mormons in a bunker under a mountain that used to be the best place to ski in the whole wide west. Even they wouldn't be able to escape the end for long.

Before the actual smoke and the real dust, the world had already gone foggy, things fading into a baseline haze. People had forgotten. People had been made to forget. People were miserable and making people miserable. There was no more right and wrong. No more good and evil. It all felt so complicated and tired and old and unclear. On that day, that last day, when the flashes went off and everything went up only to fall down, things were finally, once again, new, clear. The center did not hold. Every atom exploded all at once. And there was light. But nobody was present to see or say or pray or do anything about it. The Mormon supersoldier remembered the flash of pure, clean white light and wondered why he was still here as he stood above the girl and spoke.

He knew he wasn't the new Adam. He knew this mission was doomed, and that all the other ones, to Tonga and New Tuvalu, had been too. He told the girl that he would be back and nudged the can of corn closer to her hand. They would never see each other or anybody else ever again. Whatever he said to her, or prayed for her, or prayed to his God for her, went unheard.

There is, or there was and there is, another god here, an old god. He wants it to be known that he was here long before the first people in the Americas and their first civilization. And that he was there for all the rises and falls of civilization to follow. He doesn't know this is the last one. He thinks he will roam the earth forever and eventually rise again when humans do and once again study whatever befell their ancestors and once again use the same knowledge to find and to destroy. He hopes there will be nothing written left by the time the survivors' descendants get around to studying stuff. The first people here, the Olmecs, had no written history, none that remained beyond a few controversial glyphs, so the scholars centuries later gave him the names God II or Maize God. But he can be called upon without words. He doesn't have a name. He doesn't need one. You can find him in Veracruz, carved out of stone, surrounded by growing corn, his face that of a snarling jaguar. He is almost never depicted with a body. He doesn't need one.

You can find him again written about in the histories of the Triple Alliance, the Aztec empire, where he went by the name of Centeōtl. Before the Catholics arrived with their conversion fever and their different understanding of gods, the Aztecs knew what he was. Not *a* god at all really, but a

THE END

Teotl, "essentially power: continually active, actualized, and actualizing energy-in-motion . . . It is an ever-continuing process, like a flowing river . . . It continually and continuously generates and regenerates as well as permeates, encompasses and shapes reality as part of an endless process" (*Aztec Philosophy: Understanding a World in Motion*, James Maffie). In the cities they cut out hearts in exchange for their protection almost every day. Sacrifice was an average part of life. Mostly they killed in the name of other Teotls, like Tlaloc, who would bring rain in exchange for the tears of children, or Xipe Totec, "Our Lord the Flayed One," who demanded the hearts of warriors, or Quetzalcoatl, the serpent, who accepted butterflies and hummingbirds. Still, he knew what it was to have true power over people. He lived in hearts and minds and actions and thoughts. He was everywhere. People sprinkled drops of their own blood around their homes, and in exchange he granted them bountiful harvests of corn. He knew what it was to be truly worshipped, even after the Spanish destroyed his temple and a few centuries later put up a parking lot. Even after the Spanish came with their True God, he remained.

You could find him in almost everything there was to consume, in the years before the end. With none of their blood coming to him, he came into their blood. He was not quite edible, but they ate him up. He let them turn him into syrup.

His revenge is sweet to him, though not to the girl. She can't taste. She has no tongue, it's turned to dust, like the earth itself, and most everyone else that or who ever lived on it. She's only this alive because she was by what used to be the mountain, and now she's the only one still there besides some dogs with no eyes and the disappearing figure of the Mormon supersoldier.

There's no one left to witness, no one left to narrate, but there is corn. That's the old god's revenge. America and its world is all blown up, and this is his land again, while it lasts, but it won't. Nothing will. The rest cannot be told, but here we are. No more words. No more world. Something has to happen next. Something always happens next, or at least it used to. Girl lays in dust. Mormon supersoldier steps over her or her body. Dogs howl in the distance, from somewhere so far away that it's almost nowhere at all. This is all the distance now. Soon there will be no more soons. Soon there will be no time, no past, no present, no future. Soon there will be no space, no here or there, no right or left. Nothing will be left, not even corn.

What happens to this girl next? There's no answer. What happens to the girl next is that there is no answer. Someone has to make it up, make it happen, make it matter. Once Someone made everything from nothing. But Someone is gone now, not dead or starved to death but maybe just done, fed up or maybe He's ready to start over. Waiting for the last of this, the rest of it, to end. For the old gods to drop dead with the stray dogs. Maybe this is just one of His days of rest. It's been a while since that last one.

There's a theory that this has all happened before and will all happen again. This might be a universe made up of an eternal series of oscillations. Each begins with a Big Bang and ends with a Big Crunch. In the interim, the universe expands for a period and civilizations rise and fall and people domesticate and worship corn and dogs and gods and pray and ski and tell stories and this goes on for some time, before the gravitational attraction of matter causes it all to collapse back in on itself and undergo a bounce of some sort and begin again, again and again.

First-person-present mode activated, sorry. There's no one to look at me. I'm not here, but was anyone ever really. Who knows. There's no one here to answer. This is the last time there will ever be a now. I am the first-person present tense, here for the last person as they turn to dust. Last-person present. It's a return to form, for dust is form or we are formed from dust or it is to it that we shall return.

If I was ensouled and had fingers and a written language to write in, more than glyphs, and the center had held, or if the atomic rupture had been mended through science or the rapture delayed through faith, or whatever it was that happened had not happened, maybe I could have made a story. And in that story, this sentence would loop and twist around like a warm snake, like a perfect knot, tied to choke the truth out. Instead I can only howl. I have no words. It wouldn't have mattered anyways. This is where the story ends; the end.

Halloween Forever

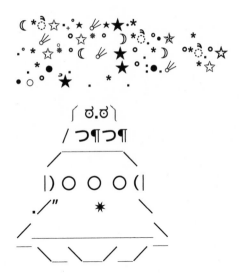

Warning signs:

- A toddler babbling "Don't forget to subscribe" as he is put to bed, because he watches so much YouTube he thinks it means "goodbye"

- Drone strikes on weddings

- Someone saying "Wow this feels like *Black Mirror*"

- A woman with a mask made of her own braids over her face to hide from security at those Hong Kong protests

- Tupac's hologram headlining Coachella

- The very normal entries nestled amid the racism on Dylann Roof's blog

- A *60 Minutes* episode on cyberwarfare that scared your grandma

- Those photos of Amanda Seyfried sucking Justin Long's dick on a canoe after her iCloud was hacked

- Kids flying drones in the park but not kites

- Mark Fisher's suicide and all those memes

- CAPTCHA (Completely Automated Public
  Turing test to tell Computers and Humans Apart)
  so convoluted it makes you wonder if you're a robot

- Mark Zuckerburg testifying before Congress with
  a face like wax

- That painting of Icarus drowning

- The growing familiarity and comfort of Amazon
  Alexa's female voice

- Twitter account @Israel tweeting about 6 free
  months of BetterHelp therapy "to those affected
  by the war in Israel"

- Our filtered faces staring back at us

I know what I look like: old, blonde, fat, as a cat, painted in
oil, and dead. I don't want to be old, blonde, fat, a cat, painted
in oil, or dead, but I'll give my face to any new app that offers
me this sort of service. I can't care where the data goes. I can't
make myself feel afraid. I used to be afraid of the dark. When
I was a kid terrified of hallways and parking lots I smiled into
every security camera I saw. I also licked parking meters and
talked to ghosts, but I grew out of those completely by the
time I reached double digits. I still instinctually nod to every
security camera I see. This isn't some *1984*-type instinct. It's
just who I am.

When I was young I didn't nod. I smiled and I showed my teeth. In the elevator or at the bank I would look right into the little orb, grinning as wide as I could. I knew it was a camera, but I didn't picture someone watching on the other end. I just liked to smile at cameras. It was like smiling at myself, but easier. Giving away my data is easy too. I imagine myself as data rich, like Kylie Jenner rich, youngest billionaire ever rich, like infinite data to spend on infinite things, enough to give away to every security agency, data mining operation, shadowy corporation. Is my data like oil or like love? Is it going to run out or can more always be made? I trade in my face for other versions of my face. Here I am with a longer, cartoonier tongue. Here I am as a man. Here I am as a clown. Here I am with a rainbow dripping out of my mouth. Here I am as a medieval portrait subject. Here I am with no eyes. Here I am with your face on mine. Here I am and I am and I am.

Here I am and here she is. She smells like pumpkin spice hand sanitizer. We've only just met, but we're drunk girls and it's the bathroom and it's a party so for this brief moment in time, we're the bestest friends in the whole wide world. She has vampire teeth and we're taking a selfie in the mirror. On her phone, through this filter, our faces are freckled, our lips plumped, our ears pointed. We're elves and we're so beautiful. I tell her that I wish it was Halloween every day and she tells me that soon enough it will be.

Halloween is scary, but so is everything else. Is that why I'm having no fun this year or does this party at a Bushwick bar just suck? Feeling haunted is no longer reserved for these late October nights of pumpkin carving, a truly absurd activity, or breaking into the graveyard on a freshman year dare or any other classic stupid traditions that allow fear to be conjured up and even controlled. I get goose bumps every day and have bad dreams every night. I have no good reason to be scared of anything, but I am often struck with a quick and horrible feeling of terror that runs up my spine out my head and says in a sharp little whisper, *Be careful, I am warning you something bad is coming, it's called tomorrow and tomorrow and next week and next year. Something bad is coming. You have been warned.* This flutter of fear is the only Halloween tradition I have left, and it is not a group activity. My lightning moments of doom are just for me, like these selfies I take with hearts for eyes. Just for me, and whoever needs my data of course.

Blind dumb fear is startling, but I am familiar with the feeling and nothing familiar can really be more than a feeling felt. It doesn't change me. I wish it did, then I could be a Greta Thunberg or a David Hogg, who are noble in their fear, like I imagine the tiny soldiers marching across Europe to the Holy Land in the Children's Crusade of 1212. It's just the ozone has always been thinning and forests are always on fire and the market has always been free. I understood that the world was ending back when I still licked parking meters. My world has always been ending just like everyone else's. We are all familiar with the wars that never end and the elections that change nothing and the climate changing everything. We should be terrified, but in the harsh headlights of approaching doom, no matter how slow or fast we think it is coming, we are stuck, like the paralyzed deer that just stand in the road and then make our lives there. The headlights still approach little by little, but the doom becomes as familiar and constant as the sunrise. We will die before the sun does. This comforts us, just as we know we will be dead when the doom collides with our deer body on that road. We won't feel the impact. We will already be nothing more than a light stain on the pavement. Stagnation scares me. Forward motion does too. Life is scary, always true, always will be. There's nothing else to try besides getting familiar with it. There's just too much to be afraid of. Lab-made diseases, school shooters, student loans, fentanyl, aspartame, cops, robbers, Russians, Americans, racists, being racist, living, dying, becoming, unbecoming, you, me.

In the bathroom, through the mirror, on her screen, this girl and I become elves. In the future, we will be elves on the dance floor and the subway. She was right—it will be Halloween every day. AI transmogrifications and filters will be real or more real or reality will be less real. We will all have some sort of little eyeball lens that communicates with other people's little eyeball lenses and changes faces in real time. This is what the boy from Stanford dressed as a cowboy tells me as he takes a Jell-O shot. When I see you, you will appear as you want to appear. It's the *next step* in beauty and identity. Makeup will be over. I like yours of course, but I usually don't like being reminded that girls spend time painting their faces.

I laugh because "painting a face" sounds so old-fashioned, something a cowboy would really say. My laugh makes him smile and turn pink as he adjusts the red bandana around his neck and swings the lasso attached to his belt. It reaffirms his masculinity to swing it around, counteracting his blushing moment.

I bet he feels really good about how he's appearing right now. I bet he wishes he could always be wearing cowboy boots with spurs and that sexy wide-brimmed hat, all authentically Western and vintage. He tells me he got them in Wyoming, where the west is still wild, and the buffalo roam freely yet cautiously, as if they know what happened to the people who lived there among their ancestors before the cowboys, saloon girls, pioneer families, and railroad men arrived to conquer America's frontier. Those people turned what they saw as an empty terrifying void of the total unknown into cities and states using their quick wits, raw democracy, rugged optimism, and radical individuality. The Stanford cowboy could go on and on with this list of adjectival phrases. He must repeat them to a lot of girls at a lot of parties. There's no point listening to his boring road trip adventure if the stakes are this low. I could kiss him and raise them, but a little shiver of fear stops me and I say thank you, fear. You are right sometimes.

He learned a lot, road-tripping back East after graduation, all alone with no cell phone or maps. I'm too afraid to dance, so I listen with my elf ears to how the West was won and what was lost in turn and how a place of lawlessness became the place of structure and surfers and Stanford that it is today. The Wild West was beautiful, but in taming it some of that beauty was reduced to myth. The wildness of the West was lost, for John Wayne and Ronald Reagan and Clint Eastwood to search for in many a film about manifesting collective destiny while riding horses through lawless infinite space.

Wow that's crazy, I reply. I wonder if the cowboy is going to offer me cocaine. Whenever I'm high I rant about Marxist revolution, basically the way the cowboy is going on about the cowboys.

It was wild, really, really wild, he says again and again. I stare at his big silver belt buckle and wonder what real

cowboys smelled and talked like. The West was freedom, he
says, just like the internet originally was! He asks me if I understand what he is saying. He's afraid he's lost me. I laugh
because he never had me. Freedom is the stuff of dreams and
nightmares only and our free market doesn't make us free
people, but the cowboy doesn't care. Silicon Valley must have
burrowed itself deep into his brain underneath that hat. He is
probably afraid of blood, or social media, or something stupid. My drink is seventeen dollars. *Poor cowboy*, I think again
and again as I listen to his musings slur.

The internet used to be destiny we could manifest, lawless, no Gods or governors or corporations or censors. Everyone could be a sheriff if they wanted to in their own little
unmapped digital ghost towns. That's over now and the cowboy sulks for a second, his hat droops down and his phone
lights up and I almost just walk away to look for the elf I met
in the mirror, but he begins again on that "internet as the
Wild West" metaphor we all know and love. His words sound
like cursive, each syllable spilling into the next, as he says,
The Web 2.0 was a frontier. It just demanded to be conquered
and so we, or I guess like old millennials and Gen Xers, or
whoever came before us did just that.

Yes, I say. They did just that. They conquered it and then
perverted it by forcing their identities of adventure and vio-
lence and organization onto it. The cowboy nods, like my

professors do, so I go on blabbering, building some identity of an identity. My words are as fake and as real as a filter that makes my lips big and nose small. The west was about collectivity . . . but also so much about the individual's power. That's why you're so attracted to it, why you bought these boots and wear this outfit on regular Friday nights. I hope you get bored with it soon.

Damn, he says.

Damn is all there is to say, so we do some coke in the empty bathroom, just the two of us in the sort of silence a tumbleweed could blow right through. The cowboy lets me do another line and then another and another and another and another and I'm asking him if he thinks the revolution will ever come or a revolution, or any change at all? and for another line, please. The two of us finish the bag and rush back through the party to the bar. The cowboy wants to dance, but I'm too chicken so we drink instead. A lonely Freddy Krueger sits down beside me and scrolls through his Instagram feed. Things can always be worse. That's something not to be afraid of.

If a snake bit you I'd suck the venom out, he says, all hat and bandana and boots, just a levitating cowboy costume. Whatever boy was there, filling the blue jeans with skin, is gone. I can see him as he sees himself, as he wants to be seen by me. I smile at the floating hat with my pointy teeth because I am now a rattlesnake, and with a shake of my tail I make the scariest noise you'll ever hear. Back when I was a human girl who smiled at security cameras and cried at the dark, back before I'd ever even taken a selfie or known that word, I was at sleepaway camp and something happened.

The cowboy listens even though he has no ears.

I was moping around behind the cabin when I heard it rattle from the bushes. Right as I was about to run away, I stopped to listen again. It was beautiful, out of sight, but so close. I listened and I understood that it was a familiar sound, the sound of fear. Look at my fear, the snake said with its tail. How afraid I am is how afraid you should be too. The cowboy and I both come back from our filtered heavens, relieved to again be as normal as we've ever been. If I had a rattler it would never stop rattling.

The cowboy is yelling about all these beginnings beginning to begin. His words are lost in the self-conscious music and laughter and my brain's blur of ghosts. My eyes must go blank because he starts shouting all of a sudden—really trying to reach me, as if I'm on the other side of some empty great plain, to be galloped toward on his horse of drunken Stanford-educated thought. I wish there was a Technicolor John Wayne sunset for him to ride off into, but there's not. Instead he just shouts all his words and I smile with normal teeth each time he finishes a sentence with three exclamation marks that dance right out of his mouth.

When we have these lenses we won't need any screens; our bodies will be the device. You'll get to choose how I see you, for real. You could be a snake on the floor! There will be rules because there are always rules, but within these rules, we will all be our own avatars!!! The future is coming! Can't you feel it?! The rules will be fair and they will protect us!

Don't laugh!

We can write the rules! We can build this world and ourselves in it! There's so much to explore!!! I can be a cowboy and you can be my cowgirl! Being will be completely different! We will be everywhere!

Not here I hope. Thank you for the coke. Goodbye cowboy. I hope you manifest your destiny. Happy Halloween: it's every night now, forever. We close our tabs. I search the dance floor for my sweaty beautiful friends who never get scared of anything.

See you everywhere, the cowboy says as I walk away.

What's scarier, to be everywhere or to be invisible? Is to be invisible to be nowhere? Kylie Jenner, queen of the filter and the filler, is agoraphobic. She struggles to leave her big white house in the Hidden Hills. She's trapped like a ghost haunting its swimming pool, but she gets to be free when she posts a selfie. She arrives onto all our phones.

A hunter from Thespiae drowned from staring at his face for too long in a pond. They named a flower after him.

Terrorists are monsters, or at least that is what my Republican ex-step-grandpa told me. I laugh because I know monsters aren't really real, except the one under my bed of course. 9/11 is still fresh. It's Thanksgiving 2001, but I wish it were Halloween. When I grow up and I am thirteen, I get a Facebook. I friend my Republican ex-step-grandpa. He posts pictures of his golden retriever. I post funny statuses. My dad tells me not to make jokes about terrorism, not because they aren't funny, but because we are being listened to. We are constantly being surveilled. We need to watch out. You need to be careful. It's the Patriot Act and it's not for patriots, he says. What's the big deal though? I don't have anything to hide. I'm not bad. How could it be bad?

He tells me it's not bad, it's the worst, and it's the beginning of the end of everything. Every adult I know has their own beginning of the end. Everyone has monsters under their beds. My uncle has his newfound knowledge of incels. My grandma has the disappearing bees. My other grandma has the Russians. My mom thinks that cell phones are giving us cancer. She buys the whole family anti-radiation cases, but they won't protect us. My dad says there is another cancer, and it's called the Patriot Act.

A week before Halloween 2001, Congress passed legislation to strengthen national security. While children went trick-or-treating, collecting Laffy Taffy and SweetTarts in pillowcases, data collection began. Nothing was private anymore. Privacy was made up a long time ago by someone, just like filters and elves. My dad sees privacy as a right. He is afraid, but I am not because I cannot remember a time when I assumed that privacy was real. He tells me to be careful because I am being watched. I tell him that I like to be watched. I need to be seen.

Other people's moms and dads must have explained this government surveillance thing to them too. I'm sure the cowboy could tell you all about it. PATRIOT is a shitty acronym for Uniting and Strengthening America by Providing Appropriate Tools Required to Intercept and Obstruct Terrorism Act of 2001.

There's this meme about being surveilled by our very own personal FBI agents. Knowyourmeme.com explains,

> **Government Agent Watching Me** refers to a character referenced in jokes in which a person engages in

conversation with a government agent spying on them through either their webcam or smartphone. Rather than sinister, the relationship between the agent and the user is usually sympathetic and emotionally supportive.

We know that when our laptops are open someone can see through the camera. We know that no message we send is private. Scary, but funny, but scary. We do all sorts of embarrassing things and our FBI agent watches. You ate a booger. You had a boy over. You spent all night searching for the perfect cowboy hat. You put tape over your camera. You got left on read. You watched some weird Wild West porn. You made a meme about the FBI agent. They saw it. They see it all and isn't that funny? Isn't it beautiful to be important enough to be watched? The government doesn't think we're important enough for health care, but to be watched, yes, of course, they can get that taken care of. We know that power is evil, but what if its agents are not? What if they are just like us? What if they could help us with our math homework, our flirtations, our little problems? What if they were our guardian angels? What if they are truly here to protect us? What if the protection we need is as simple as friendship, the gift of witness. Would that friendship look like this?

The Stanford cowboy is outside and getting belligerent. He's breaking bottles with a gaggle of skater boys. I wonder how many people have been beaten to death with skate-boards. I wonder if the cowboy can do a kickflip. I wonder if he will ever think of me again. The vampire-toothed girl is sitting on the curb waiting for her Uber. She's alone except she's not: her FBI agent is watching. It's last call. Halloween is over or it's beginning and it's time to take the train home.

Three cops stand by the turnstile. I ask them what they're dressed up as. They tell me that they're cracking down on fare evasion. It's no fair, but that's just how capitalism works. The city would rather pay three police officers to make sure we pay to take the subway than have free public transportation. This is why I shouldn't do coke. It makes me talk to cops. No fare. No fair. The next morning, on Twitter, I see a video of hundreds of students in Chile running together and hopping over the turnstiles as two police officers fail to stop them. That's how revolution works. They can't stop us all.

On June 27, 2019, three anonymous Facebook users created the event page Storm Area 51, They Can't Stop All of Us, scheduled to commence at 3 a.m. on September 20, 2019. The description reads, "We will all meet up at the Area 51 Alien Center tourist attraction and coordinate our entry. If we naruto run, we can move faster than their bullets. Lets see them aliens." Two million people RSVPed and the event became the basis for a slew of memes. Over the following two weeks, "attendees" of the group made shitposts and satirical plans to storm the base, including one on July 5 from user Jackson Barnes that gained over ten thousand reactions. The plan reads,

Ok guys, i feel like we need to formulate a game plan, Ive put together this easy to follow diagram here for a proposed plan.

The basic idea is that the Kyles form the front line, if we feed them enough psilocybin and monster energy and say that anyone in camouflage is their step dad, and the entire base is made of drywall then they will go berserk and become an impenetrable wall.

Then the Rock Throwers will throw pebbles at the inevitable resistance (we don't want to hurt them, we just want to annoy them enough to not shoot the Kyles as often). While this is all happening, the two Naruto runner battalions will run full speed around the north and south flank, and shadow clone jutsu, effectively tripling our numbers, and overwhelm the base (red circle).

P.S. Hello US government, this is a joke, and I do not actually intend to go ahead with this plan. I just thought it would be funny and get me some thumbsy

uppies on the internet. I'm not responsible if people decide to actually storm area 51.

The soldiers of the first wave would be an array of meme
characters, the expendables, Kyles, unvaccinated children,
K-pop fans, Naruto runners, Karens, furries. Then the rest
of us would follow safely and see dem aliens. I wanted to see
dem aliens. I wanted to see what our government was hiding
from us. So did two million other Facebook users. I figured
maybe six people would show. Something like 150 actually
went to Area 51. Others had a music festival instead of a raid.
The west is no longer wild.

What percentage of a population needs to revolt in order
for revolution? Only 3.5 percent, according to the math
done by Erica Chenoweth, a professor of public policy at
Harvard Kennedy School, and that's just for nonviolent
change! "We are the 3.5 percent!" I imagine the internet people shouting as they made the west wild again and stormed
the base.

Couldn't we really have pulled it off if we tried? Isn't that
why the Air Force characterized the event as a possible hu-
manitarian crisis and issued an official warning telling people
not to come? But at the same time it was silly, Halloweeny,
having to do with outer space rather than politics. I imagine
some intern being called into a secret meeting, deep in the

bunker, to brief government officials on what Kyles and Naruto runners are. I imagine the generals and strategists trying
to wrap their heads around these meme concepts. I imagine
their relief on the day of the raid when the revolution did not
begin. I imagine the intern being promoted to FBI agent, my
FBI agent. I imagine him watching me. I smile into my laptop's camera. I hope he smiles back.

Pillow Angels

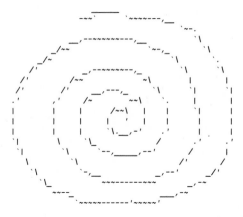

There are six lines of Vyvanse waiting on the iPad mini. One for Ottilie, one for Kaylee, one for Hadleigh M., and two for me. I already snorted so much that I remembered my entire Torah portion—וְתִשְׁמַע הָאָרֶץ אִמְרֵי־פִי: אַהֲאָזִינוּ הַשָּׁמַיִם וַאֲדַבֵּרָה—that's how good this stuff is. I could dig a hole to China and save the Uyghurs. I'd be happy to take the SAT or the ACT here on this carpeted floor. I feel like I'm Saturday morning. I've just solved the murder of JonBenét Ramsey. I can't tell you who did it. I can smell the 5G in the air. The whole world tastes like Pop Rocks on my tongue. Getting high is so fun. We're going to stay up all night. No one is the boss of us.

Ottilie says she wants to take Greta Thunberg's virginity. I tell her that one day I'm going to fuck Barron Trump. Kaylee has a nosebleed. Hadleigh licks it up. We talk like Alvin and the Chipmunks. Our words flutter around the basement like anime butterflies on CIA crack cocaine. Nothing is funny. Everything is funny. It's all so good. It's all so bad. We don't even have our learner's permits. No one can blow our minds. We're best friends forever and ever and forever will be over soon.

Out of the girls at the slumber party, I have the newest nose. It's small and straight, just like me, but natural, and it makes my whole face just work. I got it for my fifteenth birthday. You'd never guess I wasn't born this way. As the anesthesia kicked in, the doctor told me the story of how, at my age, he fled North Korea. I dreamt of his hunger and mother and fear and worship and turnips as he cut into my face. My nose was his masterpiece, he said, it made it all worth it. The white tiger he had to shoot as he crossed the DMZ, the family he knows will be punished for generations because of his crimes, the guilt constantly dripping at the back of his throat, it was worth it now. Ottilie, Kaylee, and Hadleigh all booked consultations, not that they even needed them, but he ended up shooting himself in the face before he could fix their noses. In his note he apologized to the family he left behind and the new family he left in Santa Monica. He wrote that my nose had set him free. He had finally brought something beautiful into the world and now he could leave it. I still dream about that white tiger. I wonder who it became next.

The bathroom is a Roman vomitorium. Even though I know I know there were never actually vomitoriums in Ancient Rome. Hadleigh has her fingers down Kaylee's throat. Ottilie is brushing the enamel right off her teeth. I am staring at the clumps of Nobu and Pinkberry swirling like dervishes in the toilet. We all want to be Dachau liberation day–skinny for spring break on Little Saint James. We need a vacation because LA is like Narnia now. Climate change is real. It's always winter, but never Christmas. I celebrate Hanukkah anyway so I don't really even care. When I grow up I'll control the media or the banks, but first I'll study comparative literature or new media or Nietzsche like my brother did at NYU. College will be fun, but I'll miss my friends and our slumber party conversations and their fingers down my throat.

We are the most popular girls in school now. All the other girls are fat from the hormones in their chocolate milk or paralyzed by vaccine injuries or too busy saving up for their top surgeries to even care. The other most popular girls in school threw themselves off a bridge and into the dry LA River. They just couldn't see the point in doing anything else. Ottilie, Kaylee, Hadleigh, and I weren't invited. We still had our baby fat and braces. We watched the most popular girls in school get power washed off the concrete. I even saw a few pigeons scavenge around for pieces of meat. We had a slumber party after the funeral and we knew that somewhere the dead girls were doing the same. That's what death is, an eternal slumber party. If they'd have invited us, I know we would have gone. Thank God we were ugly ducklings. Now we are swans.

The night is dark like it always is. ISIS blew up the moon.

The tide doesn't know when to come in anymore. Surfers committed mass suicide. It was so gnarly. There was another sarin gas attack at Disneyland. This time Mickey had the masks ready for sale in every gift shop. It's still the happiest place on earth. My parents had sex on Space Mountain. Nine months later I would be the second-worst thing to happen on September 11, 2001. One second, I was a martyr, piloting a plane right into a skyscraper, filled with love. Then, there with a puff, I was a beautiful baby girl being pulled out of a soap opera actress in Los Angeles. That's a fun fact about me.

Here are some fun facts about my best friends. Hadleigh doesn't have to run the mile in gym class because she has popcorn lung. All that cotton candy nicotine she vaped in middle school turned her lungs black like a coal miner's. The Make-A-Wish Foundation gave her a wish, but she hasn't spent it yet. Kaylee bought a heart attack gun on eBay when the CIA went out of business. It's worked on every stepdad she's had. Now that they're gone we can have slumber parties at her place on weeknights. Ottilie got radicalized on a Vocaloid message board. She came to the homecoming dance with a bomb up her skirt. Someone spiked the punch and she got so drunk she forgot to detonate. It was pretty embarrassing, but we can all laugh about it now, and we'll be laughing about it all night and all the other Friday nights that make up forever.

I'm cutting more lines with my debit card when the iPad

mini starts singing some song from that Disney movie about the nonbinary prince(ss) and the talking poodle. It makes my heart beat too fast and bouncy like a possessed pogo stick. We can't figure out how to turn it off without disturbing the heaping mound of crushed Vyvanse sitting on the screen. The song is teaching us a lesson about the end of the self and eternal return. Kaylee's autistic brother is moaning from his room upstairs. He wants his iPad mini. We've stolen it to do our drugs, because all our phone screens are broken and trap the precious powder in their cracks. Kaylee's brother is a buff Boo Radley sobbing like a baby on a flight to Tokyo. He wants to be near his song. But he can't tell on us and he never will.

The undocumented night nurse has no idea why Kaylee's brother is melting down. I can hear how much she needs a green card as she attempts to cover him with a weighted blanket. That blanket is only making him stronger, Kaylee says. He's too strong. Only a stepdad can subdue him. He doesn't want the weighted blanket. He wants the song. This Vyvanse has given me the power to telepathically communicate with your little brother, I tell Kaylee. He wants you to know that he lives in hell. We all do, she says as she scampers up the stairs with the iPad mini. She's right. The song gets farther and farther away and so do the tormented telepathic waves. They turn into just ripples. I'm higher than that really high building in Dubai.

I look like Addison Rae or Loren Gray or リカちゃん. My face is beautiful. I am blonde. I am Jewish. My Bat Mitzvah was beautiful. My parents were so proud. My recitation brought the rabbi to tears. I think he could feel who I used to be before I was me with my old nose and big eyes. I gave my other life for God. Instead of seventy-two virgins, I got to be a girl from LA. At the party after the ceremony I came in flying on a trapeze. There were cupcakes that looked like circus tents and contortionists and a friendly chimpanzee named Travis. I held his hand and saw something I don't want to talk about in his eyes. Travis is famous now because he ripped off a woman's face and she had to get a face transplant and then a second face transplant because her body rejected the first. I think my body is beginning to reject this face that is mine for now. I might drink Windex. I might eat a Tide Pod. I might even just let time move as fast as it does and die an old lady with this same wrinkled face.

We think that Hadleigh will be the first of us to die. Her parents will join a class action lawsuit against single-use fruit-flavored nicotine products. They promise to still let us use her tree house as our smoke spot, but only weed allowed, no vapes. Hadleigh says I can have first dibs on her tracksuit collection. This makes Ottilie and Kaylee so mad that they start moaning in wordless yearning. Hadleigh explains that I will probably die next, so it's only fair that I get to pick first.

Everyone agrees that I will meet some tragic and sudden death, like Addison Rae did on that yacht. It's such a coincidence that I look like her. I don't want to end up like her. I guess there are worse ways to end up. I guess it's a compliment.

We are in the basement speeding toward something as we laugh and laugh. It's 3 a.m. now. The basement, paneled in wood and decorated with WWE memorabilia by so many stepdads, is now a medieval dungeon. I could be trapped down here forever. The night might never end. All this speed will get me nowhere. What if we've just been running in place? What if it's one long big treadmill? What if it's an eternal loop? A demon steals after me into my loneliest loneliness and speaks to me. I think I am crying a little bit. Everyone else is too busy practicing their one-handed cartwheels to see what I see, to feel eternity recurring.

The neon Budweiser sign begins to flicker faintly. I can smell some dead stepdad's aftershave, a manly musk mingling with the burnt toast and Silly Putty smell of 5G. The little men of the foosball table begin to play a match. I wonder which dead stepdad will win. Hell can be anywhere, but usually it's everywhere. Is that where we are speeding off to or are we all already there? I want to tell the dead stepdads that I like the way they paneled the basement, but Kaylee is chanting something in Latin and they are gone again and I am doing a one-handed cartwheel as fast as I can.

Now it's time for us to play truth or dare. I say, "Truth. For everyone. What if I told you this life we're living right now and have lived, what if we have to do it again and again and all over again forever? Every ☺, every ☹? And there will be nothing new in it, literally, and we're all specks in the hourglass of eternity and it'll never stop turning?"

Ottilie asks me what an hourglass is. I show her the emoji, ☹ ⌛.

None of them throw themselves down on the carpet or gnash their Invisalign teeth or curse me, who spoke thus. We have all experienced a tremendous moment and so we can answer: "Then I would say, you are a god and never have I ever heard anything more divine."

All the cities are on fire like the Amazon was when the Amazon still was. I'm on TikTok watching them burn. I order communion wafers on Amazon Prime. I have been trying to get better. I do primal movements and meditate. I reach འཇའ་ལུས every time. I get ketamine infusions for my oppositional defiant disorder. They make me feel like a pony who broke her leg, healing like a miracle. I'm just like Jeffrey Epstein. I didn't kill myself. The slumber party is over. The sun is rising. It happens every morning, still. This is just one of many Saturdays. The sun is up again.

THANK YOU,

Scott & Tracey Levy for literally everything, especially for reading to me every night for so long.

Scott Moyers and Ann Godoff for taking a chance publishing this book, making it all happen.

Mia Council for your patience, dedication, and insight in editing.

Eugene Kotlyarenko for the stories you've told, the stories you will tell, and your ideas about how stories should be told today, and for being the first to "get me" and make me "get it" and "make me" "make it."

Matthew Davis for making mad memories, the year of pranks, your ChatGPT login, and of course the rosary and the baptism too.

Sam Serxner for your determination, work, and words that kept me going and made this happen. Abigail Walters for representing and understanding me.

Mollie Glick for all of your hard work and help.

Jon and Polina Rafman for opening up your homes and hearts to me.

Mollie Reid, Lauren Lauzon, Christine Johnston, and Matt Boyd at Penguin Press for getting people to read this book.

Marcus Mammourian for the time we had.

Dasha Nekrasova for all the things you've said.

ACKNOWLEDGMENTS

Danny & Arlene Toback for all the stay up late, PG-13–rated movie sleepover nights and mornings at the Falcon Theatre and the stories of your long-ago teenage years in LA.

Sir James George Fraser for putting me to sleep most nights.

Lazăr Edeleanu for keeping me awake the other nights.

Brewster Kahle for making sure I'll never be bored.

Angel Hafermaas for the worlds we built together, for The Augustines, who I still remember, for becoming the first novelist I ever knew that November in seventh grade.

Patrick McGraw for our pen-pal era and getting me to just type and type.

Sam Frank for all those classic "Thank you Sam Frank" moments, being so open and giving and endlessly interesting.

Galen Wolfe-Pauly for the reenchantment that September.

Celia Vargas for eighteen years of care and love.

Olivia Rosenberg for the butterfly effect you set off with a gift you made for me, a book, that flapped into the publication of this one.

Rayna Berggren for making me unlonely and the stuff we wrote together.

Dean Kissick for taking me seriously sometimes.

Andrew Shafer for being the first.

Richard Turley for the most fun I've ever had creating anything ever.

Myles Zavelo for replying to my emails freshman year and letting me read the short stories you've been working on since then as you publish them now.

Patrick Reid for the Writers Life Tips and the warm milk that time, Bloom's Day, and all the other magic moments from our time as roommates on Broome St.

ACKNOWLEDGMENTS

Zoe Doudous and Gabriel Salomon for all the games we used to play and many more to come.

Matthew Gasda for telling me to text Mia and for making me cringingly jealous enough I remembered that I am a theater kid.

Matthew Crumplar for writing about Downtown so I don't have to.

Jane King for being the first writer I ever knew and rescuing me that August.

Sheila Noonen for the best required reading the summer before senior year.

Zans Brady Krohn for starting a magazine with me ;•P.

Sherry Kramer for teaching me that talent can be taught with technique, talk about a perception shift.

Coco Candy for the year and a half that you slept curled up on my collarbone before teaching me while I was still very young the lesson of love and loss, how they are the same and the beauty is totally worth the pain.

Ken & Jaren Levy for printing that story about penguins and keeping it for all these years.

Maia Lafortezza and Adam Friedland for calling all those times, never giving up on me, giving the best pep talks.

Willing Davis for being willing to publish me.

Caroline Calloway for the title of this book (sort of) even though it's a bad choice SEO wise, which I only know because of something you once said (not to me) so thanks for that too.

C. S. Lewis, Edward Gorey, Betty MacDonald, Ursula Le Guin, and Terry Pratchett for the read-aloud bedtime stories of my childhood from before I learned to read.

Tonya Hurley, Neal Shusterman, Mary Downing Hahn, Francesca Lia Block, and Jason Pargin for the read alone past bedtime under the blanket stories of my tweens from before I learned "what to read."

ACKNOWLEDGMENTS

Peter Vack for being one of the first people to read this book.

Kaitlin Phillips for ever even speaking to me in the first place and guiding me.

Freddy & Roger Lunt for the summers in Oregon that let me learn to think and the education that I put the thinking to use during.

Rob Scharlach for all the help with aesthetics and friendship.

Jordan Castro for editing me and doing it all first, 1.0 mode.

Lukas Heller and Nicky Zou for letting me grovel and being so cool.

Giancarlo Ditrappano for supporting my book before it was a book.

Dagsen Love for being an inspiration.

Jenny & Laurent Doudous for love.

Jim Archer, Heidi Archer, Ethan & Elise Archer for all the holidays.

Angelicism01 for your words that changed me when I needed it most.

St. Michael the Archangel for defending me in battle against the wickedness and snares of the Devil. For protecting from The Hat Man.

The Hat Man for always showing up, in the corner of my eye.

Jensen Davis and Gabe Appel and Vita Salvioni Guttman for friendship.

Gabe Kates Shaw for D&G and DMT.

Walter Pearce for the fun while it lasted and more to come.

Sam Wolfe for ever and ever.